BLACKBURN DIVIS

The tranquillity of Clehonger, a close-knit Hereford-shire village, is shattered by a brutal murder. Annabel Neilson, the victim, was an attractive widow apparently universally loved. Or was she? When it comes to an investigation, the villagers clam up and for all their sophisticated city ways, Inspector Powell and Sergeant Smith cannot get any of their suspects to say anything of any significance. Even Scotland Yard cannot break through the wall of silence. There are of course, the obvious motives for them to consider: jealousy, rivalry, fear of strangers. And there are plenty of men with secrets to withhold: unhappy men seeking solace else-where and would-be adulterous husbands, the ubiqui-tous local poacher, and the whimsical Irish Roman Catholic priest.

But after a thorough investigation, all are in the clear and gradually village life returns to normal. Then, thirty years after the event, there is a confession and it looks as if Clehonger's long-forgotten crime may finally be solved . . .

Noel Green was educated at Hereford Cathedral Public School and subsequently went to commercial school for two years. He served from 1933–1936 in the Grenadier Guards, during which time he saw two years' active service in Egypt. He then attended the Northern University and matriculated in 1938, before embarking on theo-logical training. A successful career followed, which has seen him hold many varied posts: he has been curate in three Liverpool parishes, army chaplain, Rector of Iron-bridge, Chaplain of Merit to the Bishop of Chester and Vicar of Frodsham for 23 years. Now retired, he paints, teaches oil painting, and writes. *Silence* is Noel Green's second work of fiction; the first, *The Broken Triangle*, was published by The Book Guild in 1995.

SILENCE

Noel Green

The Book Guild Ltd
Sussex, England

07211883
RAWTENSTALL

This book is a work of fiction. The characters and situations in this story are imaginary. No resemblance is intended between these characters and any real persons, either living or dead.

The Book Guild Ltd
25 High Street
Lewes, Sussex

First published 1997
© Noel Green 1997
Set in Baskerville
Typesetting by Raven Typesetters, Chester
Printed in Great Britain by
Athenaeum Press Ltd,
Gateshead

A catalogue record for this book is
available from the British Library

ISBN 1 85776 198 7

ACKNOWLEDGEMENTS

I am deeply indebted to Sylvia Christie for her professional help and advice. Also I am very grateful to my proof-readers, Canon Joe White and Brenda Connelly, who gave many hours proofing the work.

Without their assistance I couldn't have written this novel.

1

The officer picked up the ringing telephone.

'Good morning. This is the Hereford City police. Can I help you?'

'Just a minute, Constable.' She took the telephone away from her ear, 'Is Inspector Powell in, Alice?'

'I don't think so, Betty. He shouldn't be long. The fog will hold him up a little.' Betty got back to the telephone.

'I'm sorry,' she said, 'he's not here yet. The fog must be delaying him. Is it very important, Eric?'

'What?' she almost shouted down the telephone. '*Murder?*'

'Just a minute, he's here now.'

'Powell here. Murder you say, Willis? When? ... A filthy night it was, too. Don't let anybody touch anything, I'll be there as soon as I can get the squad together. Stand at the door and no one, you hear me, *no one* must be let in.'

Powell was used to carrying responsibility on his broad shoulders. He looked what he was, a leader of men. He stood six feet two inches tall. His eyes were blue-grey and his dark hair was thick but always tidy. He had been one of the team 'wingers' of the Hereford police rugby team. Whenever he got the ball few could catch him as he dashed down the wing to touchdown. He was proud of his position in the Hereford police force. He was always smartly turned out and he expected those under him to look the same.

As he replaced the receiver he told a member of the office staff to find Sergeant Smith for him.

'There's been a murder in Clehonger, Leslie.' He called his sergeant by his Christian name when he was in a good

1

mood. 'Someone else will have to take over the robbery case,' and this pleased him. 'Go and round up the forensic and we'll get out there. Thank God the fog is lifting.'

Willis started telling the Inspector on the telephone, 'The postman found her at 7.30 this morning. She'd opened a shop in the village some months ago.' Powell cut him off, 'We'll find out more when we get there.'

By the time they had arrived at Hazel Chalet the fog had completely gone. As the chalet came in sight they could see people standing around in groups on the road in front of the building. They seemed to be talking in undertones. It was after 10.30 a.m., but by that time most people in the area and beyond knew what had happened.

Ted Banks, the postman, had given a second-by-second commentary of how he found her dead body. He had now told his story several times and each time another important detail came to light.

'Her body was stone-cold and there was no pulse. I knew she was dead but her eyes were wide open. I was so shocked I was trembling all over. I'll have to go now on my letter round, I've been here far too long already.'

Ted Banks was centre stage, an opportunity not to be missed. He'd never experienced such a situation before and probably he'd never have the chance again.

Another man who'd retired to Clehonger from Birmingham said to George Lewis, 'I remember that policeman from a few years back. 'He's done well, he 'as.'

George was attracted to the speaker by his Birmingham accent.

'I was just saying I've worked alongside that policeman when I worked in Bristol. He's got quite a reputation for details.'

Inspector Powell said to Sergeant Smith, 'These people are not all like Ted Banks. Mind you, he's only saying what people want to hear.

'Our most difficult task is trying to get the information out of people who don't want to commit themselves to accuse one of their number,' said the inspector, more to himself than to his sergeant.

2

'Suspicion can be a dangerous thing. They could be laying the blame at the wrong person's door,' the sergeant replied. 'Hard facts are difficult to find but that's what we've got to get somehow. Country people have a tendency to look upon strangers with an element of suspicion and fear. This attitude makes it difficult to carry out our enquiries. What they might be holding back could be much more important than what they are telling us. I've learnt a lot over the years,' Powell remarked.

'Nothing's so queer as folk,' the sergeant said.

'I can understand their fear,' said the inspector, 'If a policeman came into the village or even on Gorsty Common they'd soon know he was there and be wondering what he was there for. They don't feel the police are there to protect them.' Smith said in agreement.

All who lived on Gorsty Common thought Eric Willis ('our policeman from Kingstone'), was a friendly chap. He didn't run his neighbours in but the people in Madley didn't like Eric Willis any more than the people on Gorsty Common liked Ivor Andrews, the policeman in Madley. The city police found it difficult dealing with the country people who somehow have a clannish attitude towards people they don't know.

Neither did the people on Gorsty Common know that Inspector Powell was a stickler for details. Even when he was known as Trevor Powell, as a schoolboy, he always read the little bits in the paper: the one paragraph or short note giving some snippet of information that most people didn't bother to look at. Perhaps a day or so later the item was worthy of more space with a more noticeable headline and someone might remark about it to him and he'd say, 'Oh yes, it was mentioned in the paper the other day.' The other person would be very surprised. 'Are you sure? I didn't see it.' 'Yes it was mentioned in *The Telegraph* only a small bit at the bottom of page five three days ago.'

His mother told a friend, 'Everything in his room at home had its place and he knew exactly where to put his hand on it.' He had been given another name by those under him. When he inspected his men he noticed everything. They learnt the hard way, if anything was wrong he'd see it. They referred to him as 'Hawk-eye'.

Bristol was a good place for him to turn his academic knowledge into practical application. One town is much the same as another when it comes to crime. He decided that he wanted to join the Crime Investigation Department. Eventually he was accepted and he soon found his niche in life in the police. Now he was an inspector in that department attached to the Hereford force.

As Trevor Powell passed PC Eric Willis he thanked him for doing a good job keeping the hungry hacks out. Several newspaper photographers begged him to let them take just one picture. Powell was pleased that he had kept them at bay. The inspector gently pulled back the sheet which covered Mrs Annabel Neilson's bruised face. He saw two pennies on her eyes. He didn't know until later that Willis had put them there.

When Willis arrived he was soaking wet with sweat. His face was bright red and he was out of breath. He had carried his seventeen stone the three miles in record time. Ted Banks looked like a little boy by the side of this huge man.

'Stay at the door, Ted, and don't let anyone in. I won't be a minute.'

Willis went to look at the body. He was a tender man and had been quite upset by what he saw: A beautiful girl dead and only partly clad, with blood all over her and her bright blue lifeless eyes wide open. He had fished out two pennies and with gentle care closed her eyelids and put the pennies over them. That was how the inspector found them.

Trever Powell felt very sorry that she had met her death so young. As he stood looking down at her he spotted what looked like the edge of a black notebook half hidden by the sleeve of her nightdress. He said nothing, but picked it up in his handkerchief and put it in his pocket.

Sergeant Smith found a case with five knives. One of the set of six was missing. That could be the murder weapon, or was the inspector clutching at straws?

Eric Willis was very uncomfortable standing round and

waiting for his inspector's command. He did his best to look as if he was the most important official there. At last he was called.

'Willis.'

'Yes, sir?'

'Go and tell Mrs Banks that I would like to see her husband when he comes home.'

Ted Banks returned home at 3 p.m. Bessy gave him his meal and then she made him wash and shave and put on his Sunday best suit and his highly polished shoes which he wore on special occasions. This was quite a different Ted who pushed through the dwindling crowd to enter the inspector's office, now established in Hazel Chalet.

He was ushered into the inspector's presence to the words of Policeman Willis, ''Ere 'e be, Sir,'

The inspector had a worried look on his face. His men were still looking for the murder weapon and as yet it hadn't been found.

'I'm glad you've come to help us with our enquiries,' the inspector said, giving him a rather strained look.

'Please sit down. 'I have here...' He started looking through a pile of papers on his desk. 'It was here a minute ago.' His hands were moving faster now. 'Here it is.' It was quite a relief finding what he searched for from such a large pile of statements on the desk in front of him. He held it up for Ted to see.

'This is your statement you gave Officer Willis this morning and which you signed. I'm going to read it to you in the hope that you may think of something to add.'

Every now and then Powell looked up at Banks who nodded his head to affirm what he had read.

At the end the officer asked, 'Is there anything you could add to this? What might be of no importance to you might be a great help to us. For instance, you said you arrived at the house at 7.30 a.m. What made you notice the time?'

'I 'oped she might offer me a cup of tea but it was a bit early at that time of day. That's why I looked at my watch. If it had been about 8 o'clock I would have been all right. That's the time she makes, sorry, used to make a cup of tea and I'd have one with her.' The postman went on, 'I thought it a bit funny the door being open and no answer to my call. It just didn't seem to add up, that's all.'

'You're right there,' said Powell, 'Anything else?'

'No, not that I can think of,' said Ted.

'Did you see anyone about?'

'No, it was quite foggy when I left home at 6.30 a.m. By the time I reached here the fog had lifted quite a bit. It could have been quite thick in the night.'

The inspector weighed up the man before him as one with a sharp and very alert mind. Some said he had quick eyes like a stoat. He wouldn't miss much.

'I suppose,' the inspector went on, 'everyone dealing with the public collects enemies. Did you ever hear anyone criticizing her?'

Suddenly Ted's expression changed as he replied, 'I wouldn't think anyone round here would have done it. She was well-liked. I don't believe she had an enemy.'

'She was very attractive,' Powell said.

'Perhaps some dirty bugger tried to rape her,' said Ted, 'Was she raped?' he asked.

'We don't know that,' said the inspector. 'Well, thank you for coming in and confirming the statement you gave to the officer. I might have to call upon you again.'

'Mrs Taylor, the postmistress, might have heard something,' said the postman. 'People talk in the post office. She was the first person to find out Mrs Annabel Neilson's name. The house had stood empty for over twelve months and needed doing up and altering. Walter Taylor did the work. Mrs Taylor might be able to answer some of your questions.'

'Thank you, Mr Banks. Every bit of information is of value and could help us to find the murderer. Thank you for your help,' said the inspector.

'If I think of anything I'll let you know.'

'That will be very helpful.'

When he had gone Powell said to his sergeant, 'Our visit to Mrs Taylor could be very interesting. She sounds like a chatterbox. There's no doubt that she'll pick up lots of gossip. Our problem is sorting out the good from the bad.'

'I don't think Banks'll tell us much more.'

'Did you notice how his expression changed as he answered my question about enemies? They don't tell on each other,' said the inspector, 'but they have their opinions which they keep to themselves. Mind you, it could be a local person. They don't know if it is one of themselves. Secretly they probably have their suspicions about one or two.'

'They've got to be careful,' Les Smith said. 'Unless it can be proved, it is better to be silent and keep their suspicions to themselves.'

Sergeant Leslie Smith was the ideal assistant to Inspector Powell. The sergeant could grasp a situation. He saw the whole picture. He made notes of his findings and thoughts for future reference. He also took notes for his boss in another book. As a policeman, he took a general view, while the inspector, as an artist of investigation, took particular interest in the little things which made up the whole, like the Victorian illustrators who took great care over the details which made the picture much more interesting. A mountain was one thing but put a man fishing on the lake and the whole picture comes to life.

The inspector worked from the details to the whole crime and the sergeant worked from the crime to the details. They made an excellent team. They often irritated each other with their stance but their thinking was complementary.

The evening had come and they discussed their next line of enquiry. Inspector Powell tossed a black book over to the sergeant. It looked like a notebook.

'What do you think that is?'

Leslie picked it up and looked at it.

'We've got the fingerprints, there are three of hers and two of another person,' said the inspector.

When he opened it he couldn't read it because it was in a foreign language.

'What language is this and where did you get it?'

7

'I think, no I'm pretty sure that it's Latin. But you'd never guess where I found it,' Powell said. 'I had a peep at the body before the doctor examined it. I'm glad I did because I found it just showing under her arm. It probably belonged to her. She was a devout Roman Catholic and it could be a sort of prayer book. It looks well used. I'll ask Father O'Hara next time I see him.'

The sergeant handed it back with the remark, 'Interesting.'

'Perhaps tomorrow may be a more profitable day,' said Leslie Smith. 'There's no sign of a knife yet but the doctor did say that it might not have been a knife. The stab certainly looked bigger than a knife wound.'

'Our first big problem is to gain the confidence of these village people,' said the sergeant.

'The trouble is that they don't trust each other and so there is little chance of them trusting complete strangers like us,' said Trevor Powell. 'People who moved here twenty or thirty years ago are still looked upon as foreigners. The murder, by comparison, is a straightforward procedure. To break down their suspicion of "foreigners" trampling over their private lives or to try and tear apart their loyalty to each other in the parish is quite another thing,' Powell said.

'We'll have to take it one step at a time,' Smith said.

'We'll interview all the people as their names come up,' said Powell.

'We'll get a lead if we're patient,' the sergeant remarked.

'I wish that we could find that bloody knife.' The Sergeant knew the knife was worrying the inspector. He felt that it was holding matters up until they found it.

Now that the shock was subsiding, the reality of what the brutal murder meant was sinking in. Everybody felt under suspicion. They were suspicious of each other and the police were not looked upon as friends but as enemies trying to pin the murder on one of their number.

The inspector was to learn that when trouble comes the local people cling together. They profess to know nothing, neither have they seen nor heard anything. The only way out of the dilemma is to say nothing about anybody to anybody. It becomes a tight-lipped community and it was going to be a difficult task to break the barrier down. It was with some trepidation that Powell viewed the task before him.

PC Willis had been standing round like an out-of-date law book most of the day. The monotony was only broken when a reporter or a photographer had tried to get in to see the remains. The cameraman wanted a picture. But Willis had his orders and he made sure they were kept.

Now the place was flooded with officialdom: several policemen of various ranks, police photographers and the fingerprint men. The police doctor pronounced Annabel Neilson dead and gave a time of death somewhere between 11.00 p.m. and 3.00 a.m.

Now it was the end of a very busy and important day for the local policeman. Inspector Powell and Sergeant Smith were still talking.

'When they've gone,' Constable Willis said to himself, 'I'll be glad to get my feet up.' The mist swallowed up the police car as it went on its way to Hereford and as he peddled home he said to himself, 'It's a queer business. No murder weapon, nothing stolen. The doctor said she wasn't raped and there's no fingerprints of the visitor. I'm glad I'm not the inspector.'

Eric Willis was happy to be going home. He'd had enough for one day. It was freezing and the constable knew that mist would cover everything with the white lace of hoar frost by morning.

2

The woman who'd bought the wooden chalet in Hazel Lane had quietly moved in. The for sale notice had stood there so long that the weather had worn the wording away but now the board's absence attracted people's attention. The old board was lying face down on the unkept garden.

'What's her name?' asked Ted Owen.

'I don't know,' said Will Pearson. 'She's a good-looker and very smart.'

'I wonder where she comes from. Is she married?'

'P'raps she's divorced and doesn't want her husband to find 'er.' Will Pearson mused.

'Could be, there's some things we'll never know.'

'I'll ask the boss, he'll know,' said Ted.

'P'raps she's single and writing a book and came here for peace and quiet to write it,' said Will.

'Don't let your imagination run away with you, Will.'

'Course, she could have a married man here and she's come to be near him,' said Ted.

'Listen to who's talking! Any more bright ideas?' Will asked.

'Anyway, she won't have paid a lot of money for the place, I don't suppose,' said Ted.

'It looks a bit rough on the outside,' Will said.

'I wouldn't expect it'ud be much better on the inside either but it's well-built.'

'I expect her'll start doing it up a bit come spring.'

It was not only the men who noticed her. The women with

10

critical eyes had also tried to weigh her up.

'What's a smart attractive woman like 'er from out of the blue come 'ere for?'

There was no answer to a multitude of questions.

The first bit of information had come when Annabel Neilson had gone to see Mr Taylor, the local builder, to see if he'd do some work for her. He had a very attractive blackboard outside the post office upon which was written in gold leaf:

WALTER TAYLOR
BUILDER AND UNDERTAKER.

His wife was the postmistress, a job which suited her inquisitive nature. Taylor's workshop was behind the house, back off the main road. Walter had given up building houses for quite a while but he did odd building jobs, specializing in house repairs and roofs and there was a steady but small turn over in funerals. Joe Morgan, the official rat-catcher, would always dig a grave out when Walter asked him.

It was Saturday morning when Annabel called at the post office to see Mr Taylor. Mrs Taylor came to the counter a little breathless. She was a big plump woman, whom Annabel thought to be in her late fifties.

'Good morning, Mrs Taylor,' she had said. 'It is Mrs Taylor, isn't it?'

'Yes that's right,' she had answered, with a smile.

'I'm Mrs Neilson from the bungalow in Hazel Lane. I've really come to see your husband if he's in.'

'He's about somewhere. I expect he's in his workshop. I'll give him a call,' Olive Taylor had said. She wanted to get him into the office so that she would know why the woman wanted her husband but Annabel had stopped her just when she'd filled her lungs to shout.

'Oh! I'll go to the workshop, don't you bother. I'll find him.' Olive was thwarted, but she was one up on the neighbours. She knew the woman's name and it wouldn't be long before they'd all know. It would be a talking point for her customers. Olive had been very anxious to know what Mrs Neilson wanted her husband to do for her. She asked him the minute the woman had gone.

Getting anything out of Walter was like trying to get a snail out of its shell with a pin. Walter never was very forthcoming. He knew that whatever he told her would soon become common knowledge.

He had been sawing a piece of wood and he hadn't seen or heard Annabel come in but when he'd looked up what he saw gave him a very pleasant surprise.

'Good morning,' he'd said. 'I'm sorry. I didn't see you come in.'

As he spoke he'd been looking her over with his experienced eyes for measurements. She was about five foot eight inches tall with dark brown hair and a beautiful figure and lovely legs. He thought that she was about forty one or twoish. He always thought that it was such a terrible waste when he went to take the measurements of a woman with a lovely face and figure that he was going to bury in the ground. His Olive had given up the struggle of keeping trim a long time ago.

'Well Mrs . . .'

'Neilson,' she'd said.

He'd noticed that she had a wedding ring on her finger and Annabel thought that he had an eye for detail. She was right. He was a good craftsman and proud of his work.

'What can I do for you on this lovely morning?'

'I live in the bungalow in Hazel Lane. If you could come and have a look I could show you what I want done.'

'Yes, I can do that, Mrs Neilson, When would you like me to come?' Walter had asked.

'I go to church in the morning but I could see you tomorrow afternoon. Could you manage that?' Annabel asked.

'I also go to church morning and evening. I'm a churchwarden at the parish church. Funny,' he said, 'I don't seem to remember seeing you.'

'I'm a Catholic, Mr Taylor, that's why you've not seen me there.'

'Oh, I'm sorry, Mrs Neilson. I can come tomorrow about 3.00 p.m., if that'll suit you.'

He noticed that she looked straight into his eyes as she spoke to him. There's nothing shifty about her, he thought. She held her hand out and he took it. It was soft and warm. It was a genuine handshake, not the wet lettuce kind.

'Tomorrow then, at 3.00 p.m.,' she'd said.

Olive had been looking in that direction ever since Annabel left the office. She could hardly wait for her to go. She was dying to know.

When Annabel had gone, Olive came to the workshop door and asked, with a sweet coaxing voice, 'What did she want, dear?'

'She wanted some work doing on her bungalow.'

'What had she got in mind?'

'I can't tell you.'

'Or won't.' Olive snapped.

'Now, there's no need to be like that. I don't know what she wants until she shows me.'

'Oh, she's going to show you. When?'

'I'm going up there tomorrow afternoon at 3 o'clock.'

'I'll come with you. It'll be a bit of an outing for me. I'm stuck here seven days a week.'

'Very well, dear. You realize that this is not a social call. It's business. I don't think you'll find it much of an outing.'

'On second thoughts I think you're right. Perhaps another time, dear.'

Walter Taylor had made a point of being punctual. The vicar at church was very strict about time. He, as churchwarden, had to be strict and now he did the same thing in business. On the stroke of 3.00 p.m. he knocked on Mrs Neilson's door.

Annabel welcomed him in and when they were seated she explained to him what she wanted. Walter did a rough sketch of the general layout of the place. It was like a train carriage, one room leading into another. When she shut the front door she turned right, leading the way to the sitting room. They went through one room which was used as a dining

13

room, with a large lean-to kitchen off to the left. From the dining room they entered quite a large sitting room with two big windows giving plenty of light. The windows looked out on the front garden and path from the front door to the lane beyond. Looking left in the room there was a big stone fireplace. The deep red curtains, together with a cheerful coal fire, made the room warm and cosy.

'The chalet is much bigger than it looks from the outside,' remarked Walter.

'The room behind the fireplace is the master bedroom,' Annabel pointed out. 'It has a fireplace using the same chimney stack. There is another room off the sitting room which is the last room in that direction.'

It had all been carefully worked out. The living quarters, together with the WC and the bathroom, which was placed between the two bedrooms, were all near the heat centre.

'Someone spent a great deal of their time planning all this, it's been very neatly worked out,' said Walter Taylor, who would appreciate the mind behind it.

'I want to show you Mr Taylor what I want done.'

Annabel led the way back to the front door.

'This is the part of the house I want making into a shop. This first room on the left, together with the hall, could be used as a shop, with a long counter opposite the door and display shelves behind. The far room will make a good store room. What do you think?'

'I think the plan is very good. I'll take some measurements and I'll make a few notes now. Then I'll draw up some plans for you to see and I'll come and see you in a few days.'

'Thank you, Mr Taylor. There's just one thing. I don't want the information to get out until I'm ready to open, so please don't tell anyone. It might create some bad feeling even before I get started.'

'A bit of competition never did any harm,' said Walter.

'I want it to be surprise.'

'I understand,' said Walter. 'No one will get a peep out of me, Mrs Neilson. I'll block out this part of the house so that no prying eyes will see what work I'm doing.'

'Thank you. Would you like a whisky or anything?'

'No thank you, I must be going. It'll soon be church time. Many thanks all the same.'

Annabel Neilson had recently lost her husband and had come to Clehonger to start a new life in a new place. Her parents had been shopkeepers and she had been brought up in that business atmosphere. A friend took her to see the place. As soon as she saw it she felt that everything was right about it for the purpose she had in mind, including the good position on Gorsty Common. On the wooden gate at the entrance she could just read the name, 'Hazel Chalet', which she thought was a very pretty name. The parish was slowly opening up, especially hereabouts, and she was sure that business would develop. It was going to cause quite a stir on Gorsty Common. Now the local people would have a choice. The other shop, often referred to as 'The Gold Mine', would lose some of its glitter. Annabel didn't seek confrontation but the people in the area thought that there'd be a price war.

It was going to bring competition and also it would produce an undercurrent of resentment by the other shop. She fully expected some unpleasantness and she was sure that she would be accused of causing trouble.

Apart from the business, Annabel was a very charming lady with a lovable personality. She both attracted the children and brought a new interest among the menfolk who came to her for their cigarettes and tobacco.

On the great day of opening Annabel only had three customers, One was Mrs Bessy Banks, the postman's wife.

She was very cheerful and chatty and passed off the lack of Annabel's business by saying, 'Most people don't know you're open. When they know they'll come a running, have no fear. They've paid top prices for years to the Thomas woman. She'll have to watch what she's charging from now on.'

'Well Bessy, there'll be no fancy prices here.'

Annabel felt a lot better after her chat with Bessy.

It was Friday night and pay day and the Plough Inn was always busy over the weekend. It was very noisy and people had to shout to be heard. Many local people came for a pint and a chat.

Fred White and Joe Morgan were sitting at a table with Mrs Maggie Bowlan and her quiet husband, Will, joined them.

'Budge up a bit, Fred,' said Joe, giving him a gentle push. 'Now, Will, sitie down. What are you two having, it's on me.'

'Thanks, Joe, 'alf of mild, please Joe.'

'Will?' Same please, Joe.'

'Where's your dad, Fred?'

'He's stopping at 'ome tonight, he thinks he's got a cold coming.'

'He's in the best place, it's 'ard throwing a cold off this time of the year.'

'Well, Joe,' said Maggie, 'what do you think of the new shop? I feel it's part of the village now.'

'I reckon it's the best thing we've 'ad since the electric came. We've got more variety and some things are a bit cheaper for us now,' Joe said.

'She's a very nice lady, who only wants to earn an honest living. Her parents were shopkeepers in Ludlow when she was growing up and she's used to working in a shop. I can tell you one thing, she's not interested in any kind of war and that includes a price war. We were talking about it in the shop today,' said Bessy.

'We've 'ad enough of wars without 'aving private ones as well,' Mrs Bowlan affirmed.

'The chalet makes a good shop the way she's arranged it and it's 'andy where it is. I 'opes she continues doing well,' Fred said and the others agreed with him, saying, 'Hear, 'ear'.

It had been noticed that the children on their way to school very seldom passed without going in for a pennyworth of sweets.

'Annabel Neilson loves children. She loves to see the happy smile on their faces when she gives them a few extra sweets for their penny and the parents appreciate her generosity,' said Maggie.

Will Bowlan summed it up by saying, 'The new shop is good for all the people living round here.'

Maggie thought she'd got him talking but he never said another word all night.

To the casual observer, nothing would seem significant about a man walking with two dogs but those who were friendly with Joe knew what these dogs were used for. They were whippets and that told you a lot about their owner. The dogs weren't just a poor man's greyhounds but special dogs for the poacher. To see Joe Morgan no one would think that this innocent looking man could be a thief. He was like a cat, all friendly and harmless during the day but he turned, like a cat after dark, into a murderous fiend as far as the rabbits were concerned.

Strangely enough when he called at Annabel's shop she was very taken with him. He was tall and in his late thirties, she thought, with dark hair and big blue-green eyes.

He gave her a cheerful, 'Good morning. I think it's going to be a fine day.'

'I hope you're right – I've some washing to get out. What can I get you?'

'Have you any St Bruno tobacco?'

'Yes, I should have. I sold Mr Lewis some yesterday, do you know him?'

'Oh yes. I've started doing some gardening for him. The ground's a bit heavy, and will be for a while. He's got a lovely bungalow on Birch Hill. He'll know a bit more about living up there when the wind starts to blow.'

'He seems a friendly sort of fellow,' Annabel remarked.

'He's proper 'Brumigum',' Joe said with a laugh.

'You're lucky. This is the last packet of St Bruno until the new delivery comes in next Tuesday.'

'I'll last out till then,' he said as he paid her.

While he was talking he was having a good close up view of Annabel and he liked what he saw.

'Would you like a rabbit sometimes?' he asked.

'Yes, that would be nice.' Annabel flushed with pleasure as she answered.

17

'I'll draw him for yer.'

'Thank you very much, that really is kind of you.'

'If you want a pheasant or a wild duck just let me know, I can get you anything like that.'

'Thank you very much, Mr Morgan.'

'Please call me Joe,' he said. 'Everybody calls me Joe.'

She thanked him again. This time she called him Joe and gave him her attractive smile.

He may be a poacher, she thought, but he's a very handsome one. Two days later Annabel found a parcel on the doorstep and when she opened it she found a skinned rabbit all ready for the oven. I will give him some tobacco next time he comes in, she thought.

Others didn't see Joe in quite the same light.

'He's as crafty as a fox. You've got to be good to catch him. When they did catch him it was more by good luck than good policing,' Eric Willis the local bobby admitted.

Joe found it exciting, not just outwitting the rabbits, but not getting caught himself. The secret of his success was his complete silence. The farmers and the law made such a noise that Joe and his pals knew exactly where they were, most of the time. They did get caught now and then.

'One of these days Joe Morgan will find himself behind bars,' Eric Willis prophesied.

George asked Joe, 'I've been wondering if a greenhouse would be damaged by the wind. We're a bit high up here.'

'I don't think you'd be wise unless you put up a tree windbreak but then you'd lose your views,' Joe told him. George accepted his advice. He didn't fancy throwing money into the wind.

They were getting along very well and they talked about many things including the shop and especially Annabel. They both would have fallen for her but they both agreed that chance would be a fine thing.

All the local people on Gorsty Common knew that Joe Morgan was a poacher but they didn't mind buying a rabbit or two from him because they were very cheap. They didn't ask any questions.

Robert Sadler was a poultry farmer. George got to know Rob. They always had a chat when George collected the eggs for the week. George asked him one day how things were going and Rob told him how things had changed since he was a boy.

'In what way have they changed?' George asked.

'They don't go by the breed any more, they think in terms of meat and eggs and you feed them accordingly. I buy day-old chicks and in twelve or thirteen weeks they are ready for the table.'

'Well,' said George, 'I'm learning something new every day.'

'I went to Mrs Neilson's shop the other day. I thought of you. She might sell some of your eggs. Have you asked her?'

'I wish I was twenty years younger and single I'd go for her.'

'Why bother about being single?' said Rob. 'You're in your prime at your age.'

'You'd stand a better chance than me, Rob, but she'll take quite a bit of persuading.'

'No,' said Rob, 'the look in her eyes tells me to keep off. She would be a smashing catch for the right bloke.'

Rob fancied himself with the ladies. Someone said, 'Rob Sadler thinks of himself as the answer to a maiden's prayer.' The girls couldn't be blamed, he did look like Clark Gable, the film star. He was smart and well-groomed. But the girls who worked there had been warned by Phyllis Evans, 'Don't let him get too close He'll flatter you and say all kinds of nice things to you but when he puts his arm round you and his loose hand starts to caress you, that's the time to run.'

Because Annabel Neilson had recently lost her husband, Rob thought he stood a chance until they met, then, when he looked into her eyes, he knew that she was not for him.

One day Elsie Sadler and Doris Morgan were having a chat in the shop when the loud ring of the shop's door bell announced Bessy Banks.

'Good morning all,' she said, crashing into the conversation, 'I've just seen the vicar, he's a rare sight.'

'Funny, we were just talking about him. Elsie was just saying, "Bessy, what a pity he lives so far from us".' Bessy agreed, 'But it's not his fault. I'll bet he wishes he hadn't got to live in such a big house, him being a bachelor and all.'

'On top of that,' said Elsie, "'e's got problems created by the very things we're all happy about.'

'What do you mean.' Doris asked.

'You know how happy we were when the electric light and the buses came. These things have changed people's lives. The vicar was saying to Rob the other day that people can now go on day trips on Sundays in the summer and read the Sunday papers and books by the new electric light in the winter but it's created problems for the church which no one ever thought of.'

'I never thought,' the Vicar had said, 'that when I came to the parish that I'd have a fierce battle on my hands, not against people, but against circumstances which everyone welcomed.'

The vicar had told him that the churchwardens were getting very worried because the collections had fallen quite a bit. The electric light made a wonderful improvement to the yellow twilight of the oil lamps of the past but, with a twinkle of her eye, Bessy Banks had said, 'We've lost the teenagers who used to hold hands in the back pews. They've got to be good in the bright lights.'

'You seem to know a lot about what went on in the half light, Bessy,' said Doris Morgan.

'I've 'ad my moments, Doris,' Bessy said with a laugh. 'Sometimes a girl had quite a struggle to keep the boyfriend's hands on top of her skirt instead of underneath. But it was fun and more enjoyable than the vicar's sermon. All can be seen now and so the back pews are empty. The big changes have made it difficult to meet the running expenses, which no one would have dreamt would happen.'

Bessy Banks asked Annabel, 'Is your church feeling the same effects?'

'It might be but it doesn't seem so.'

Again the door bell rang in walked George Lewis. They all said 'Good morning'.

'Good morning, ladies, what a pleasure it is to see so much charm so early in the morning.'

'Now, now,' said Bessy, 'the answer is no.'

They all laughed and headed for the door.

George had come for his tobacco and he noticed that Annabel had started selling daily papers. He had missed his *Express* but now he could collect it. He gave her an order for it and *The Gardener's Weekly* magazine. The walk would be good exercise and he liked having a chat with people. He gathered little bits of news here and there which reminded him of the old days when he was a policeman.

Joe told George that he'd been caught poaching and fined. He didn't want him to find out from someone else. News of this kind travels fast. George told him that he was a bloody fool and warned him that it would be worse next time.

Marjory Lewis had joined the WI and she also brought back little bits of news. They both had heard that Mrs Neilson was waging a price war. However, most people thought that it was a pack of lies.

'Nothing but jealousy,' said Doris Wright, Harry's wife.

Bessy Banks, the postman's wife, spoke for most people when she said, 'It's a good thing that we have another shop in the parish. It means that we now have a bit of competition and a drop in some of the prices.'

The Plough Inn was, without doubt, the best place to learn what was going on in the parish. The warm atmosphere and the real ale worked wonders on the customer's dry tongues. Much of the news that floated around was hearsay, but sometimes it was bad news and true.

3

'What'ul-it-be George?' asked Tom Walker, the landlord of the Plough Inn.

'A pint of bitter, please, Tom.'

George looked round the tap room. It was only 8.30 p.m. and customers were crowding round the bar.

'It soon fills up on Friday nights, dun'it?' George said.

'Ah, if you don't get here early it's standing room only,' said Tom.

'You can't grumble at that. With only one pub in the village, it's a real gold mine,' George commented.

'It may be a gold mine but it's bloody 'ard work getting the gold. Mind you,' said Tom, 'it's pretty slack in the week. How's that garden of yours coming on? I 'ear Joe Morgan's working for you. He's a good gardener, so I'm told, and good at a few other things on the side,' he added, giving George a knowing look.

'Oh, I'm very pleased with him. He says he'll come back in the spring.'

'I 'ear you're a keen gardener yourself,' Tom said, with a twinkle in his eye.

'Whoever told you that was pulling yer leg. Mind you, I like to see it tidy. It's too much hard work for me though. I came here to retire not to work myself to death. There's one thing for sure, the garden will be there when I've gone.'

George liked talking to Tom. The Birmingham accent was music to George's ear. As he listened to Tom he could have been back in 'Brum' in his old home and among the people he had known all his life. His lingo brought back so many happy memories.

'How long have you been 'ere now, Tom?'

'Just over two years,' Tom replied. 'Time goes so quick. I 'aven't the time to do gardening like you. I've got to work for my living,' he said with a smile on his face.

'I like talking gardening, it's a world apart. I look forward to the weekends when I have a good spell reading *The Gardeners* magazine on Sunday afternoon in the armchair. But seriously. I've never had a garden. It's all new to me.'

'That makes two of us then,' said Tom.

'I'll find me a seat before they are all filled,' said George. He spotted a table and an empty seat and asked the two men, 'Can I join you?'

'Ah there's plenty of room,' said one of the men.

'You sound as if you've come from Birmingham,' said the other chap.

'Yes, that's right. I've got a bungalow up on Birch Hill.'

'Oh ah. You've got a good view from up there, and the wind when it blows.'

George had never thought of the wind. His home was certainly very exposed.

'The prevailing wind comes over those Black Mountains,' said the older man. 'The wet southwester can be very strong at times.'

'You're from round 'ere?' George asked.

'Yes, born and bred,' said the younger one.

'That's my dad, 'Arry White, and I'm Fred. We own the petrol station and cycle shop.'

'Nice to meet you. My name is George Lewis,' he told them as he shook their hands.

'How do you like living here?' Harry asked.

'Very much,' George replied, 'but it takes a long time to get used to the silence after living in Birmingham. But apart from the fresh air and the silence that we've got for free, there's another personal blessing.'

'This sounds interesting, George. You haven't got another

woman on the side like the woman who lives in a wooden chalet by any chance?' Harry asked.

'No, of course not. I'm quite content with the one I've got. In any case, I'd need to be a bit younger for the lady who owns the chalet. No, I'm glad to get away from the competitive war which rages night and day, week in and week out. I was the owner of a bedroom slipper works. It sounds like an easy, pleasant and trouble-free occupation, dun-it?'

'One wouldn't have thought that there were many difficulties there,' said Eddie Macklin.

'As far as the manufacturing goes you're right, apart from the rising costs of the raw materials which makes an ongoing job with the books. It's the crafty way firms try to capture the sales. It's a cut-throat business, I can tell you. I've reached the stage where I am damn glad to get out of the rat race.'

'Of course, the ordinary man in the street doesn't know about those sort of things,' Fred remarked. 'The pressure of competition takes all the pleasure out of the business. I'm glad to be free of it all.'

'Quite a few of your people come from Birmingham and have settled here,' said Fred.

'I expect some of them are as glad as I am to be retired. It's to be hoped that they can stick the great change of living in the Black Country,' said George.

'Probably some of them will drift back after a while.'

'Why should they do that?' Harry asked.

'Well,' said George, 'it's a bit difficult to explain. You get used to noise and bustle, you get geared up to it and then when you move out here it's all different . . . the noise has gone. Even the smells have changed, you know,' said George, warming to his theme.

The two men laughed.

'You certainly don't get the farmyard smells in Birmingham.'

'I'll tell you what you don't get here,' said George.

'What's that?'

'You'll have a job to believe this, but in November in the city you get the smell of chimney smoke. It lies in the air and

24

you know it's November. It's a different smell from all the other smells. It's funny how you get used to things.'

'I suppose you get used to anything in time, provided you have enough of it,' said Harry.

'I can believe that,' said George. 'I'm not so sure that I have enough time to adjust to the slower way of living. Time is what I'm a bit short of.'

They looked at his greying hair and nodded their heads. Then Fred's dad added a comforting word.

'You never know, you could live longer out here. Life is not so fast. There's no factory chimneys belching out smoke and dirt. The air here is pure. Per'aps that's why folk round here live to a good age.'

'Maybe you've got something there,' George said as he got up. 'Well, I'll be off back to the missus. I don't like leaving her too long.'

Eddie Macklin took George's seat saying, 'Who's George?'

'George Lewis from the bungalow up on Birch Hill,' Harry told him.

'I've seen him once or twice. Now I know who he is. It's a lovely place he's got there. It won't 'alf catch the wind though.'

'We mentioned it to him. He said he hadn't thought of the wind.'

'He soon will,' said Eddie.

'I see they've got the footings in for another house in Eaton Lane.'

'I expect there'll come a day when Clehonger will be a suburb of Hereford. There was a time when we knew everybody but things are changing here like everywhere else, and not for the best,' Harry said.

'There's one thing for certain: it won't happen overnight so we have a bit of time to adjust,' said Eddie.

'Those who've come 'ere don't look like the type who'd want to take over the place. Most of them have come to retire and enjoy a bit of peace.'

'I 'ope you're right,' said Harry.

'We don't mind strangers coming 'ere provided they don't

try and interfere with the way we do things,' said Fred.

'I don't think you'll get any trouble here,' said Walter Smith. 'You might get the odd one who likes to hear his own voice but he won't last long.'

'We're very lucky up to now that we've got some very nice people. Let's hope we can keep it this way,' said Harry White and Fred nodded his head, agreeing with what his father'd said.

The voice of Tom the landlord could be heard above all the noise: 'Time, gentlemen, please.'

'Hazel Chalet is a good place for a shop. Mrs Neilson's doing very well. It looks a bit shabby at the moment. Old Ben Lovel kept it looking nice,' said Harry.

'How long's it been empty, Dad?'

'It must be near on twelve months since old Ben died.'

'It don't do a place any good standing empty, specially when it's wooden.'

'I think a lot of us are very happy we've got a second shop. I'm sure the prices have come down because of the competition. Mrs Neilson is a very charming lady in her early forties, so I'm told,' said Eddie.

'There you are, Fred, you needn't look no further,' said Harold with a laugh.

' 'Old on, I've only seen her once. She may be all right,' Fred said, a bit doubtfully.

'Oh, yer can't be picking and choosing. She's a woman 'ain't she? That's what you want, something to look arter yer. We'd better get out of 'ere before he throws us out.'

'Good night, Tom,' Harry shouted to the landlord.

George was getting used to roads without street lighting. Tonight there's nearly a full moon. He'd never realized how much he could see by the moon's soft light. There was hardly any movement of air. Everything seemed to be still and silent. The forming mist was gently covering everything like a fluffy blanket and there was a cold nip which made him hurry back to Marjory.

'It's cold out there tonight, Marjory, and the fog is coming down. I felt it more because it was warm in the pub.'

'Were there many there?'

'Full to the doors. It's always busy on pay day but by Monday night there's hardly a soul in sight. I was told by Harry White something that I'd not thought of. We'll get strong winds up here. I was thinking of having a greenhouse but I'm not so sure now. It might get blown away.'

'Well, George, they should know what they're talking about. This is what we have to pay if we want good views.'

'There's one thing about you, Marjory, you're a real pragmatist.'

'Is that something nice, George?'

'Yes, darling, of course it is.'

'You'd better talk it over with Joe. He'll know about the wind.'

'Yes, dear, I'll do that. I find the people very friendly and there's no shortage of advice. There is a little fear that the newcomers might want to change things but I think they've come here for a quiet life. I wouldn't want to be involved in village politics. I've had enough of it in business. I suppose you'll always get some smart-arse who'll have a go.'

'I'm glad we've got our place built. They were saying in the pub that land is getting dearer by the day. In five years or so this will be quite a large village. People are moving in all the time. There's still much interest in Mrs Neilson. She's doing very well with the shop by all accounts. Some of the people on Gorsty Common are very pleased the monopoly has gone.'

'They were trying to get Fred White married off to Annabel. I thought Fred looked a bit worried that he might be turned down. It's funny the way their minds tick, Eddie Macklin said, "she's just what you wants".'

Apparently he'd been out with one or two girls but his efforts had turned sour. Even his father was wondering what was going wrong. He was a bit like his mother he thought, he wasn't the pushing type. That's why his father hadn't retired before. Harry White, his dad, got the answer when someone said that he'd be better off with an older woman 'to gently push 'im a bit'.

They were soon to learn that the lady who had moved into Hazel Chalet had made a greater impact on the life of the people living on Gorsty Common than all the other strangers put together.

One morning, when George was buying his paper, he remarked to Annabel how well he thought she had settled in and how tidy everything looked.

'That's very nice of you, George. It looks a terrible mess to me but it will all come right before long.'

Mrs Bowlan heard that bit of conversation as she came in.

'You see, Annabel, George is a very likeable person.'

'I can see that, Maggie, but a man don't see things in a house as a woman does.'

But George could see how well-groomed she was. He had noticed how often she'd changed her hairstyle. Sometimes it was pinned up and sometimes brushed back or plaited or done up in a bun. These little variations added an interest to her appearance.

She also chose her dresses with care. There was nothing flashy about her. She was, indeed, a very attractive person. She radiated vivaciousness and other people were happy to be in her company. Many people often felt better when they had talked with her.

She was talking to Mrs Banks when she said, 'I have no room for negative thinking.'

Despite her troubles she believed that the world is not interested in the sad and miserable things. She felt that it is the future which is important. The past is only valuable as lessons on how to handle the future. If she could look at life that way then other people would be happier if they did the same. All who knew her said she was a positive thinker. Running a shop suited her outgoing character. It was her happy attitude to life that brought customers as much as the better prices of her goods.

Her husband's job as an electrical engineer had taken him to South Wales. It was here, at Port Talbot, that he had died of pneumonia which developed from the 'flu'. The job he was on was pressing and he had got up and gone to work before he was fit. They had been married twenty-four years. Bit by bit she told her friends about herself.

'I had to move. The place was too full of memories for me. I had to start afresh.'

As Bessy listened to her, she thought that Annabel had enjoyed a wonderful marriage. Bessy realized that when there's a closeness in the loving relationship the parting by death becomes much harder to bear.

'There was an openness between us,' Annabel continued. 'We discussed how we felt about things and why. We talked to one another and sorted out any problems. The same applied to our intimate relationship. An old doctor had said, "Get things right in bed and all other things will fall into place. Where there is sex as an expression of love, the bond will stay the test of time." '

'I've not had a married life like that,' Bessy said. 'We've never talked about sex, which I've always thought of as a duty and the marriage certificate is a legal contract to stop him going after other women.'

'My Ted is no leader of men, he left the leading to me. Oh, I've got used to giving the orders. I love him but more like a son whom I have to tell what to do. I've been a good wife to Ted. But no one ever told me anything about married love and sex. It was something "you found out about". My mother told me nothing only. "Don't let a boy have his way with you," but I didn't know what she meant.'

The physical part of Annabel's life came to a sudden stop and now she had no outlet for her pent-up grief and stress. Because the relationship had been so fulfilling and exciting, the loss was that much more biting. There were times, when the day's work was over, in the stillness, that tears sometimes filled her eyes but she felt better after a good cry. The marriage had rewarded her with a son. A hysterectomy had prevented more children, much to their mutual disappointment.

What with the shop and all the work it entailed, travellers calling, the replacement of stock and the bookkeeping, not to mention the housework and washing and cleaning, she had little time to look back. Every week she went to the corrugated-clad church to thank God for her wonderful marriage and to pray for the soul of her dearest Henry.

There was quite a good following of Roman Catholics in the area and so in this respect she felt quite at home. Her religion was a great comfort to her, especially now that her son had had to go away to work. He came home when he could. She knew that she could not hold him and she had no intention of developing a possessive mother's love. She had seen the heartbreak mothers suffer when their child leaves home. She knew that one day a girl would take possession of him.

The shop was doing very well and the eye-catching notice stating THIS IS A CASH AND CARRY SHOP told all the customers that there was no 'tick' trading. Business seemed to be improving by the week and Annabel realized that it was silly trying to do all the work herself. It was making her very tired.

She asked Maggie Bowlan, 'Do you know anyone who would like to work for me?'

Annabel liked Maggie. She was full of fun and always had a tale to tell. She also knew what was going on in the place and was the most likely person to know someone who might like to work in the shop. The next time Maggie called she dashed in bursting with laughter. She told all and sundry the news that the school boss had set his trousers on fire.

'However did he do that, Maggie? You're 'aving us on.'

'No, I'm not, it's true. He was sitting on the fireguard watching the children working and there was a bang and a red-hot coal, no bigger than a marble, flew out of the fire and settled on his jacket and for a while he didn't notice it. It burnt a hole in his jacket and then another hole in his trousers and burnt his bottom. There was such a rush when he realized that his trousers were burning and his bottom was getting burnt. He dashed to the water butt and sat in it to put the fire out. The class couldn't help but laugh. I'm afraid it made him very angry. It's going round that the school boss has got a roasted bum.'

30

Maggie Bowlan reminded Annabel of a bumble-bee, buzzing round here and there picking up bits of information as a bumble-bee picks up honey.

Two days later Vera Turner came to see Annabel.

'I'm Vera Turner. Mrs Bowlan told me that you are looking for some help in the shop.'

'Yes, that's right, Vera.'

'I'd like to come and work for you,' Vera said. 'I've been at the dairy for three years. I don't mind the milk side of the work. It's the mucking-out I find unpleasant and very hard work. It makes me too tired to go courting in the evenings,' she added, with a shy smile.

'This is good news, Vera, I'm delighted that you can come. When can you start?'

Vera thought for a second.

'I can start on Monday week.'

Annabel felt relieved even at the thought of the extra help. She also saw in Vera an added attraction for male customers. She was a well built young lady who was just nineteen years old. She had a very pleasing figure with an ample bosom and a trim well-proportioned body. She had flaxen hair and blue eyes. No wonder she was never short of a partner on the dance floor. Bill Maddocks, Vera's boyfriend, was anxious to marry her before someone else enticed her away from him. He needn't have worried. Vera had turned down all the others. Her two brothers could be very supportive if she ever needed them. Fred was eighteen and Tom was seventeen. Both worked as farm labourers and they went rabbiting with Joe Morgan.

Every Sunday Annabel followed a pattern of activity. Firstly she went to Mass, then she had her breakfast. Then she tidied up and did the dusting. She always had dinner at midday. Other days she had it when the shop was closed for the evening. After a rest, she checked the stock and balanced the books. After tea she settled down to read *The Sunday Express* and *The News of the World*.

31

After five months of trading she found that she was carrying stock which had a slow turn over. She decided to drop such items from her shopping list which in turn would cut down her bookkeeping.

She'd just reduced her stock intake when Vera announced, 'I'm four months pregnant but I can carry on for quite a bit yet.'

'You'll be all right provided you don't do anything silly. No reaching heavy things off shelves or carrying heavy boxes,' Annabel advised.

'The doctor has warned me.'

'That's right, dear, follow the doctor's advice and you'll come to no harm.'

'I thought I'd better tell you as soon as I knew to give you plenty of time to find someone else.'

'Thank you for telling me.'

'I don't think I'll come back when the baby's born. It's early days yet but it depends how much baby-minding my mum will do.'

'Of course. Don't worry, Vera, about those things at the moment. Now that I have sorted out the stock, I'm reducing most of the things that are not selling well and cutting the bookwork down.'

When Vera goes, Annabel thought, I don't think I'll replace her. I think I can manage on my own.

When Vera decided to finish work Annabel thanked her for all the help and they parted the best of friends.

Although Annabel was deep in the country, she didn't feel lonely. The door bell was a cheery sound, but she was glad many a time to shut up shop at 6.00 p.m. Some of her customers had bits of news to tell and she was getting to know their little ways and the kind of things they bought.

Mr Pennell was blind and she could always hear him coming up the steps to the door by the sound of his tapping stick. Then he'd tap the door and then the counter where he stopped.

'Good morning, Mrs Neilson.' He knew that she was there.

'How did you know I'm here?' she asked one day.

'I know because I can smell your scent.'

'I haven't got any on today.'

'It must be on your clothes. I can smell it.'

'Oh yes. I remember now. I tipped the bottle over and some fell on my cuff yesterday. That's what you can smell.'

'That's right, Mrs Neilson. When you lose one faculty the others become more sensitive to compensate for the loss.'

No sooner had he tapped his way out than Mrs Williams arrived. She was bursting with anger about the gypsies.

'I don't trust 'um. They'll steal anything,' Mrs Williams stated. 'They're not proper gypsies you know.'

'What are they apart from being a thieving lot?'

'They are didicois,' said Annabel.

'Didicois? Is that another name of thieves?'

'No,' said Annabel with a laugh. 'They're Irish tinkers. The true gypsies are a proud race. They are the true travelling people. The rich among the Irish tinkers are scrap metal dealers. They've no need to steal but they do, however rich they are.'

'I always feel uncomfortable when they are around. I think it must come from my childhood days. If I was naughty I was told that the gypsies would have me. I've always been wary of them. Anyway, I don't mind as long as they keep moving,' said Mrs Williams.

How fast time flies, Annabel thought. Summer turns to autumn and the autumn colours fade as winter sets in. Now it's dark by four o'clock. The winter evenings seem so long. These were occasions when she really missed her Henry. It was then that she felt the bane of loneliness. Locking the door seemed like a deliberate act to shut herself away from her friends and neighbours, who at such times were the very last thing she wanted.

She never thought that she'd welcome a late caller.

4

At 6.00 p.m. Annabel turned the key of the front door lock and pushed the door bolt home. As she walked back to the kitchen she thought that she heard a tap on the front door. She stopped and stood still.

'It can't be. I didn't see anyone about,' she said out loud to herself. The tap was repeated. 'Yes, there is someone there,' she said and she returned and opened the door.

'Good evening, Mrs Neilson.' It was dark outside but she recognized the white face and the even whiter collar. 'Forgive me calling so late. I've just left poor Mrs Jones and I thought that I'd call while passing for a few minutes.'

'Oh, Father, it's lovely to see you. Do come in.'

'Are you sure, now. I'll not be putting you out at all?'

'Of course you're not. I'm delighted to see you. How is Mrs Jones?'

'She's in bed with a bad chest cold. Her younger sister is looking after her. What with the old lady gabbling away in Welsh and her sister answering her in her language and me saying, "What's she say?" and then me getting it all again in English, it turns a short visit into a long one. When all's said and done, I gather she's an improver.'

'You must be exhausted.'

'It certainly would have been much easier if someone had taught her to speak English.'

Annabel was leading the way into the sitting room.

'Can I get you something, Father. How about a little drop of whisky?'

34

'That would be very nice, but only a little one, I don't want to be falling off me bicycle.'

'A little drop will do you nothing but good, Father. Where is your bike?'

'It's by the front door. It'll be all right there.'

As they entered the sitting room Annabel pointed to an easy chair by the fire.

'Here you are, Father, you sit there and I'll bring you your drink.'

Father Patrick O'Hara had seen this very attractive woman at church but apart from speaking to her as she left the church they really hadn't met. He very much enjoyed sitting in a comfortable chair by a cheerful fire. As he looked round the room it reminded him of his own home with pictures on the walls and pretty curtains to the windows and all the little things that make up a home. How very different from the institutional coldness he was so used to, like an outer waiting room of a solicitor's office.

'Here you are, Father.' As she gave it to him she said, 'You work long hours but this will do you good.'

'Do you smoke, Father?' she asked.

'Yes, I do, but only a little.'

She noticed that he had a slight Irish brogue. She went out of the room and came back with a packet of cigarettes.

He took one and said, 'It is the first today.'

'Have you missed your homeland?'

'No,' he said, 'not now. I did for some time when I first left but I have been away some years now. I now feel more English than Irish, apart from my accent, of course.'

He looked to be about in his fifties and his hair was going grey. He was the parish priest for a very large parish. His flock were well-scattered around Menbolt Abbey, which was a few miles from where he was sitting.

'Come to think of it, all the Christian religions are well-represented around here,' Annabel said. 'There's the Church of England, our Catholic church, a Methodist chapel, a Congregational chapel, a Baptist chapel and a Presbyterian chapel and they are all well-attended. Robert

35

Perkins, the vet, said, "The local church people are spoilt for choice, going from one church to another. I reckon they've got a bad attack of foot and mouth disease." '

'The vet must be a bit of a comic,' Father Patrick commented. 'It's better to settle and learn a bit of discipline. When I came to England I had to learn to live here. If God wanted me to work here then I had to control my desires and not be going back to Ireland as often as I could. My home and my people are here now. Those people who can't settle are really unhappy. I only go home occasionally, just to see my parents. But I'm fully adjusted to the English way of life. I have been at Menbolt for the past six years now and I know all my people in the parish.'

Annabel was very pleased to see him. She had only ever said, 'Good morning, Father,' as she left the church on Sundays. Now she felt that she could talk to him. She told him all about herself. There was no other person she could talk to about her happy marriage and how much she missed her Henry. She didn't feel shy. She told him how she missed the sexual expression of their love.

'Maybe I'll get married again. There're times when I feel I couldn't remarry. But the other times, the longing is almost more than I can bear. I don't find praying about it helps. It just increases the desire. I keep very busy. I have so much to do, which is a good thing. It's only in the silent moments that my thoughts turn inward. "Saved by the bell" has a special meaning for me. The bell is the shop bell and someone's coming is to help me change my thoughts.'

She was glad that she had told him about her longings, so he would know what trials she had behind that smiling face. She knew that he could understand the feeling of loneliness and the problems she had to carry.

He held her hand and reminded her that 'God is good and will give you the strength you need.' He handed her his handkerchief to wipe the tears on her cheeks.

'You will feel better now that you have unloaded your burden. We'll carry it together. I will pray for you.' He got up. 'Well, I shall have to be going. It's getting on towards

8 o'clock and soon it will be time for compline,' he told her. 'I'd like to call again if I may,' he added.

'Please come any time. You'll always be welcome, Father.'

She let him out and thanked him for calling. His visit had shortened the night a little she thought as she closed the door and turned the key in the lock. As the lock clicked into its bolted position it seemed so loud, like an audible full stop at the end of a sentence, as much as to say, 'That's where the friendship will stop.' Now all was silent again. It was at such moments that she missed Henry to talk to. How quickly the time passed when the priest was here, she thought. There was so much unsaid. She admitted to herself how much she would have liked to be held in his arms, to have the comfort of loving arms round her. He seemed so gentle and kind. But it was wrong to think like that. Why are some temptations so sweet and irresistible? His musical Irish lilt lingered on in her mind and filled the silent moments.

She was not to know, even the wish was too much to hope for, but it was to be the first of many visits he made during the long winter evenings.

Suddenly her mind was jerked back to the present by another knock on the door. She looked at the clock, it was half past eight. She said to herself, 'Now, who can this be?'

As she opened the door she saw a pale-faced elderly lady with a worried look on her face.

'Hello, Mrs Richards, are you all right?'

'Yes, dear, I'm really sorry to bother you at this time of night but I've run out of tea. Would you let me have a packet?'

'Yes, of course, Mrs Richards. Come in. Which kind do you have?'

'Brooke Bond will do very nicely. Thank you again. I'm so sorry to have troubled you.'

Annabel wished her good night and again she shut the door gently and, turning the key in the lock, hoped that such visits didn't become a habit with some people.

The following week Annabel found another parcel on her

doorstep with a dressed wild duck inside. She knew where it had come from but she had to wait to thank Joe when he called in for something from the shop. He did call just before closing time and so she asked him if he would like a drop of whisky?

'Yes, thank you.'

'Are you having one?'

'No, I won't if you don't mind. I have a drop sometimes before I go to bed. The doctor says it's good for you in small doses.'

As it had just turned 6 o'clock, she turned the key in the lock and led the way into the kitchen and pointed to the room beyond.

'You go and sit down, Joe. I'll just pop the potatoes on the stove. I won't be a minute.' Then she came and sat beside him.

When she'd opened the door and seen it was Joe, her heart had given a little flutter. She liked Joe. What a pity he was married, she thought. She could love Pat or Joe and would like to be loved by either of them but they were both committed. There are times when I'd like to think they could be free to express their love and I could return it without it being a sin, she fantasized.

As she came into the sitting room she asked, 'Tell me Joe, why do you go poaching?'

Joe laughed.

'I go for the hell of it. It's the gamble of getting the rabbits without getting caught. That's the fun of it, it's not the money. We don't do any damage and the farmers are always bellyaching about the damage the rabbits do and yet they hate our guts for helping them keep the numbers down.'

'I must see to the potatoes. I won't be a second.'

'I'll come with you. I like the kitchen.'

'Oh, very well. We can sit just as well there.'

'That suits me fine,' Joe said.

'Have you been caught?'

'Oh, yes, I have but it does not stop the excitement. I don't like snares. I think they are cruel. The poor things get caught

38

by a leg and they nearly pull their leg off to get free. Sometimes it's days before they are put out of their misery. We don't use guns, they make too much noise.'

'I'm glad you don't use snares. They wouldn't be so bad if they killed them off at once but they don't. Thank you very much for the duck. I'll have it on Sunday for my dinner.'

'They're not very big, but it should be enough for a good meal.'

'What does your wife think about your poaching?'

'Not a lot. She doesn't say much but she gets very angry if I get caught and I'm afraid we have a hell of a row. The money I get from the rabbits I put into a separate fund. I call it my "Nick" fund. As long as the fine is reasonable I can pay it out of this fund. Getting caught doesn't happen very often, thank God. It's getting an expensive business. They take all my tackle and fine me. Then I've got Doris to face. The way it's going, I shan't be able to afford my fun soon.'

'Do you think the risks are worth the kicks, Joe?'

'I keep saying it's time I stopped before I get sent to gaol.'

'I'd hate that to happen to you, Joe. It's not fair on Doris either. If you went to gaol she'd be very upset.'

'Yes, I suppose you're right, Mrs Neilson.'

'Please call me Annabel. I feel I've known you for a long time.' She stood up saying, 'I shall have to get my dinner now.'

'I shall have to be going too,' he said as he rose from his seat. 'Thank you for the drink.'

She was quite pleased that he had called. He seemed a little shy. She felt that she would only meet the real Joe when he was not so shy.

The next time Father Patrick O'Hara called he told Annabel a little about himself.

'I was born on a small farm in County Clare. I was the O'Hara's third child. The first child died under peculiar circumstances. They found him dead in his cot. It was a terrible shock and no one knew the cause. Even the doctor was mystified. He said that he had heard of this happening but that it was rare.'

'The medical world is still trying to find out how it happens. It certainly must have been a terrible shock for your parents,' said Annabel.

'Yes it was. It was a long time before they got over it but inside they never will. The second son, Benedict, was now the heir and would inherit the farm and so my brother is the farmer and now I was the one who would go into the church. It was a tradition in those parts for one son in the family to go into the priesthood. The Roman Catholic bishop lived in Ennis, which was about five miles away. There was no village where we lived, just scattered farms, a mile or two apart.'

'You must have felt very lonely and cut off.'

'No, not really. We played together when we were young and we had a dog and, of course, there were always the little people. They danced over the bogs at night with their little blue lights. Some people don't believe in them but I do. I've seen them dancing in the dark. Our teacher used to tell us about them: the good ones, the fairies and the elves and the lands beyond the sea where the saints go. He used to tell us about the bad goblins and the magic of the pixies. Religion, magic, angels, fairies, saints and goblins and the mystery stories of the other world across the sea were all woven into one.'

This was something Annabel had never thought of before. Sometimes he would have that faraway look in his eye. A dream-world of saints and fairies, fact and fiction, magic and mysticism were all part of the fabric of his religious faith.

'No, we were never lonely. The angels, the little people, the cheerful pixies and the saints like St Anthony were always helping us to find things we had lost. We knew that they were around us all the time.'

Annabel sat in wonderment. He believed it as he believed the Holy Bible. What a childlike faith.

'All the land is boggy and only the local people knew the safe paths through. Such knowledge is vital. People who didn't know could be swallowed up in the bog. The grass looked so green and inviting but if you didn't know the paths through the bogs you could disappear.'

'Did you ever get frightened that you might lose your way?'

'We always carried a long stick so that if we were uncertain we could probe the ground and we carried a lantern to help us see and, more important, that others could see us, so if we were in trouble they'd know where to find us.

'I had to cycle the five miles to Ennis for my schooling. Here, at this stage, I was struggling with my Latin. Soon it was to become the language of my daily worship. I found the theological training long and hard. I enjoyed the solitude round the farm where I could wander off and revise my theology or history or philosophy. When in the town of Ennis I would look at the girls and there were many times when I would have liked to take one out but I had to remember that they were not for me. I was already married in spirit to the church. Sometimes I wanted to rebel.

'My young sister was my nearest contact with the opposite sex but I didn't learn much from her about women and, of course, nothing about sex and human love. I got some love from my mother but that was a different love.'

He could not tell Annabel all the experiences he'd had as an army Chaplain. He just said that he had joined up as a chaplain in 1942.

'When the war was over I came here to England and I have been here ever since.'

'What a fascinating story, Father.'

'When we're together, please call me Pat. I find it more homely. I like calling you Annabel.'

Father Patrick had never told the whole story. He daren't. He saw a lot and learnt a great deal as a chaplain in the war years, especially in France. Sex and prostitution were commonplace, like seeing dead bodies or badly wounded soldiers. It was surprising how he had become hardened and accustomed to these things. He was then thirty-two years old and there was a part of life he hadn't touched. He was a man before he was a priest. He had natural desires which at times he felt the church had cheated him out of experiencing. The rule of chastity did not stop the natural urges which other men gladly satisfied. Most of the time he was too busy with

41

the sick and dying to think of these things.

Once or twice he had the experience of the forbidden fruit with a French prostitute but he always felt badly about it afterwards. However, the stresses of war and bodily tensions subsided after his visit to a brothel, which did him a lot of good. Though he had experienced the physical act of sex, it was only part of the real fulfilment. It was sex without love. He longed for sex as the expression of love. He knew that he had not taken part in the real thing. What he had experienced was only the shadow of the embodiment of love.

Several times he was at war with his church for forbidding marriage but he firmly believed that there was no salvation outside the church he was in. Now he was in the dangerous fifties and the urges he had lived with seemed to be intensifying. He found Mrs Neilson very attractive. He felt a warmth there, not as with the cold prostitute, where it was purely business. However much he tried to put such thoughts out of his mind, the more they persisted. He felt that he was caught.

His church said 'No', and his whole being said 'Yes'. The battle raged inside him. It was no good, he would have to call again and face the temptation on its own ground. When he called it seemed that Annabel was pleased to see him.

'Hello, Pat, come in. It seems ages since you were here last. I think that you are doing too much. This is such a large parish that you could do with another priest to help you.' She looked quite concerned as she said it.

Pat felt the warm atmosphere of a caring love. It was a wonderful experience he'd never had before.

She didn't know how he was feeling about her but she knew how she reacted to his presence. His being there comforted and excited her. What a pity he was a priest. She really could love this man, she thought.

Neither spoke of their inner feelings but they talked round the subject.

'It's difficult to explain how much I miss the love Henry gave me. He would hold me in his arms and tell me how much he loved me. I can hear his words now,' she told him.

Even talking like this made her feel that she would like to

be in his arms instead of sitting on a chair apart. He spoke of his loneliness of heart and the barrenness of affection.

When he got up to go he held her hands and gently kissed her forehead and thanked her for being so frank with him. They both realized that their thoughts mingled into the oneness of understanding. Were they falling in love?

Annabel had a restless night. Thoughts kept going through her mind like water through a sieve. She was attracted to Joe. He was not a brutal man. He even cared for the rabbits. He didn't like them to suffer pain. He was tall and strong, a real countryman and she could nestle up in his arms. Doris is greatly blessed with such a man, she thought. Oh, how I could love him . . . but there was Doris. Then there was the whimsical captivating appeal of my Irish priest, she told herself. He needs love and affection, someone to care for him.

But first there was the big question which loomed unanswered in the silence. Would he leave the church if he fell in love? Would he marry her?

'I would marry him,' she said to the full moon which shone through the bedroom window.

She tried to control her thoughts which were jumping about like a frog.

And then she thought, there's Fred.

The first time Annabel saw Fred was on a Saturday morning when she was going to the Post office to see Mr Taylor. He was putting petrol into his car but he was looking at her and smiling and she smiled back. He had sandy hair and bright blue eyes. He stood about five foot ten inches tall and had big broad shoulders like a boxer. It seemed a long time ago now but she found it difficult to forget.

Harry, his father, who had just turned sixty-eight years, had made up his mind to retire and give Fred a free hand to expand the business. Fred spent many hours planning what to do with the business. He'd decided to have another big shed built where cars could be repaired. The petrol pumps and cycle shop were on the main road and motor cars also needed attention and he was in the right place to service them.

Ever since Harold Smith, the schoolteacher, had mentioned Mrs Neilson in the pub his thoughts turned from work to romance. He made a point of getting to know her. Every day he called and bought *The Daily Mail* and one day he thought he'd try to get her to have a meal with him in Hereford.

Fred was no romantic. He was just a practical well-adjusted man needing a wife to run his home, raise his family and give him the comfort which he needed to save him straying after other women. He spent a lot of time thinking how best to put his proposition to her.

This wet and dark morning seemed the most propitious. No one else was in the shop. This was the time and in his hurry what he had to say didn't come out the way he'd planned it but the message was clear.

'How would you like to come with me and have a meal in the Mitre Hotel in Hereford? They serve a good meal.'

'That's very sweet of you, Fred. Yes I'd love to do that sometime.'

Fred was not going to be brushed off.

'How about a week tomorrow? That'll be the sixth of December.'

She thought to herself that Pat comes on Fridays. She also knew that Fred was interested in her. The invitation confirmed that.

'Yes, Fred, I think that I can manage that,' she said. 'I shall look forward to that very much.'

Fred was so pleased that he nearly tripped over a bucket full of tablets of Life Buoy soap as he made his way to the door. Annabel and he laughed as they returned the soap to the bucket.

That night Annabel lay in bed but couldn't sleep. So many things passed through her mind. She switched back to her shopping list. 'I mustn't forget to order some more candles and fire lighters,' she said to herself and 'it's no good lying here,' she thought. 'I'll get up and make a cup of tea.' The clock said that it was a quarter to one. As she drank her tea she made a list of the things she had to order from the salesman from Goldings. Her mind turned back to Pat and his childlike faith. 'What kind of a woman have I got to be to break down church barriers and Irish folklore?' she asked herself.

'Oh! forget it,' she said aloud. 'You're as bad as Pat, living in a world of make believe. It's time you went back to bed. You've a busy day tomorrow.'

This time she went to sleep. When she opened her eyes the moon had gone and heavy dark clouds filled the sky and, to make it worse, it was raining. She'd had a bad night and she was still tired and wanted to turn over and go back to sleep. She looked at her loud-ticking clock by her bedside. It was 7.30 a.m. Another day had started.

When Fred came for his paper she was pleased that he was the only person there.

'I'm looking forward to our dinner date,' she said.

Annabel had not been out with anyone since her Henry died. It was a real treat. Going out for the evening was quite exciting in itself.

'I've booked a table for a week tonight,' he told her, 'and we'll go in my new car. Come and have a peep. It's in front by the gate.'

There was no one to be served so she went out with him. The Morris Oxford was gleaming because it was new and also because it was raining. He opened the door on the passenger side for her to get in out of the rain.

'Oh, Fred, it's beautiful.'

'I am glad you like it. It's better than going by bus.'

'It most certainly is. I find it most exciting.' And she gave him a kiss on his cheek. He gave her a rather shy peck on her cheek in return and went off to his cycle shop happier than he'd been for a long time.

Annabel now had three men interested in her and she thought of them all in different ways. She felt that she could lead Joe, but not Fred. She was sure that she could be happy

45

following Fred. She found it difficult to compare Pat with either Joe or Fred. She felt that she could walk hand in hand with Pat.

Pat was calling on Annabel on Tuesdays and Fridays. She thought it wise to cool the relationship a little with Pat and so on the Friday she said she had a bad headache. Pat was very sympathetic and didn't press her. He left early, which was something he wanted to do if he could tear himself away from her. Just as he was leaving she told him that she was going to Vera's on the following Tuesday. She told him that she couldn't get out of it.

Annabel wanted to stand back and look at her situation.

5

Annabel was very strict about opening and closing times. Her father had always been strict about this. He had said, 'People rely on you to be open when you say you'll be open and when you say you'll be closed at a given time you'll be closed.' She felt that she couldn't do that when people called after hours. She thought, there are mornings when I might as well not have bothered and this morning looked like one such day. It was gently raining and misty. However, Fred had come early for his paper and she had sat in his new car for a minute or two. Apart from that all had been quiet.

At last the bell on its curled steel spring clanged as someone opened the door and before it had time to stop its clanging rhythm it clanged as someone shut the door as he or she came in. Even if she had been in the garden she would have heard it, especially when everything was so still and quiet. Even the birds were silent.

Annabel looked at both her clocks. One said two minutes past nine and the other said nearly five minutes past nine. She didn't know which clock was right. Neither one was far out. She had just finished the washing-up and she left the dishes all wet and glistening and went into the shop as she dried her hands.

'Good morning, Mrs Haines. You're about early this morning.'

'Good morning, Mrs Neilson. I'm baking this morning. My sister's coming this afternoon so I'm going to be busy,' said Mrs Haines.

'Your sister hasn't picked a very good day, has she?'

Mrs Haines always looked prim and proper. She had been a schoolteacher before she married and she still kept up the teacher's image.

'Have you heard about Bob Evans?' asked Mrs Haines.

At that moment Mrs Pugh came in and shook her umbrella before she closed the door.

'What a terrible morning,' Annabel said.

'It is indeed,' said Mrs Pugh, 'and it doesn't do my chest any good, not to mention the arthritis.'

She, in contrast to Mrs Haines, was plump and fussy. Life was trying for her with all her aches and pains.

Mrs Haines started again now that her audience had doubled. She still acted and reacted as a schoolteacher giving her children a lesson. She didn't like being interrupted when she was speaking. Again the door bell rang and in came Phyllis White. She started again.

'Have you heard about Bob Evans?'

'No. What's he been up to?' both Mrs Pugh and Annabel Neilson asked, almost in unison.

'Well, I've heard that he was down in the Bines with Walter Clarke yesterday. Bob tried to jump the brook and slipped and broke his leg.'

'He ought to 'ave known better at his age,' said Mrs Pugh.

Mrs Haines pressed on despite the interruption.

'He couldn't be moved in case he did more damage and he was in terrible pain. Walter had to come and fetch Mrs Morgan to put his leg in splints. Walter thought that as she was used to laying out the dead, she would be the best one to get. It was half an hour before they got to 'im. It's quite a distance and they were out of breath when they got there. He was in a bad way. It's a good job that Mrs Morgan brought some whisky for him. It brought a bit of colour back into his cheeks.

'Mrs Morgan was the only one Walter could think of at the time but it was a wise choice. She found two boards and some bandages and got Mrs Bennett from next door to come with her.'

'By the way, how is Mrs Bennett?' chipped in Mrs Pugh. 'I hear she had a nasty fall.'

'Oh, she's all right now,' snapped Mrs Haines.

'Anyway,' she went on, determined to finish her tale, 'they put the splints on him and made 'im as comfortable as they could so that it wouldn't be too painful when he was moved. In the meantime, Walter got Bill Morris and two of his fellows to get him 'ome on an old door out of the barn and Mrs Bennett, under orders from Mrs Morgan, went to the post office and got Olive Taylor to ring Dr Foster.'

Mrs Taylor, it seems, had rung the Kingstone number and the doctor had answered the telephone. Dr Foster lived in Kingstone but he had a very large practice covering several parishes. To say that he lived there is hardly true. He seemed to spend most of his time travelling from one patient to another, not counting emergencies. He did eat and sleep there and he had a very busy surgery two mornings a week.

He was a dapper little man 5ft 3ins tall with red cheeks and a fair complextion. He was now in his fifties and beginning to lose his hair but not his memory. He knew all his patients by their Christian names. His cheeks were rosy red and they got redder and redder as he went on his rounds by pony and trap. Everyone loved him and most knew his tipple. That was why his colour was so bright. He liked his drop of whisky. a little drop here and a little drop there all helped to make the work a little easier. By the time it was getting dark he gave his pony a free rein and the faithful nag took a tired but blissfully contented and snoozing doctor home.

It so happened that it was surgery morning and the last patient had gone. The nurse had just tidied up when the telephone rang. She heard part of what was said.

'Hello, Dr Foster speaking.'

'What did he do a damn soft thing like that for?'

'Oh, she did, did she? Well, Sarah's all right.

'Now listen, Olive. You tell Sarah that I'll come as soon as I can. I've only just finished surgery. When I've had something to eat I'll come and see him.'

'Yes, yes, he'll be all right. Tell Sarah to give him a drop more whisky if the pain's too bad. Goodbye, Olive.'

Mrs Foster and Alice, the maid, collected Billy, the pony,

from the paddock and fastened him into the shafts of the trap while the doctor snatched a bite to eat before starting off. He arrived soon after 1 p.m. His poor Billy had run all the way but the doctor was quite refreshed by the pure clean air after being so long in the surgery.

Sarah was waiting for him in case she was needed.

The first thing he said to Sarah was, 'Have you got any of that whisky left?'

'Yes, Doctor.'

'Bring two glasses then, one for Bob and one for me.'

The doctor poured a stiff one out and handed it to Bob.

'Get that down you,'

The doctor didn't let him drink alone. He poured the same amount out for himself. They both felt better after that.

'Now let's have a look at it.'

The doctor was very gentle. He knew how painful it was, even to the touch.

'I'll try not to hurt more than I can help.'

He had brought the district nurse with him and he handed her Mrs Morgan's splints.

When he'd gently examined the damage, he said to the nurse, 'It's a simple fracture of the fibula.'

'You've bust your leg, Bob, and we've got to put it in plaster. What the hell were you doing?'

'That'll teach you,' said Dr Foster, 'to remember at fifty plus not to behave like a chap of fifteen.' He went on to tell him, 'It'll take its time, I'll see you in a week.'

As he was going out he said, 'You'll be able to move around a bit in a few days.'

'Bob Evans will certainly go through it for a while, but with all the pain there was one good thing,' said Dilys Pugh.

'What's good about it, Dilys?' Mrs Haines asked.

'He'll lose some weight which he can well afford,' said Dilys.

'His trouble is that he acts before he thinks and I don't suppose it'll be for the last time,' Phyllis White said.

'I'm sorry poor Bob's had an accident. He was coming to

do my garden next week. Now I doubt if it'll be done at all this year,' said Annabel.

'Why not ask Joe Morgan to do it?' said Mrs Haines. Annabel's heart gave a little flutter when Joe was mentioned. 'He's not doing much at the moment. Our local rat-catcher doesn't overdo himself. He could fit it in, I'm sure,' said Mrs Haines.

'If you see him will you ask him to call?' Annabel asked, having regained her composure.

'Yes, I'll do that, Mrs Neilson, if I see him.'

'What can I get you, Mrs Haines?'

'I want a loaf of bread, a quarter of tea, a tin of Nestlé's condensed milk and some hairpins.' She looked at her list. 'And a two pound bag of self-raising flour, please.'

Annabel collected her orders and put them on the counter for Betty Haines to put in her bag.

'That will be three and eight pence altogether, please.'

Mrs Haines fished the money out of her purse with finger and thumb and laid it out on the counter.

'Thank you, Mrs Haines, it's just right.'

'I'd better be off then, rain or no rain,' and the bell rang twice as she opened and then shut the door behind her.

On her way home Mrs Haines met Joe.

'Mrs Neilson wants to see you.'

'What have I done now?'

Mrs Haines laughed.

'You've got a guilty conscience? She'll tell you,' and Mrs Haines hurried on out of the rain.

The shop doorbell rang again. Annabel was quite pleased that the miserable weather had not kept the customers away.

'Hello, Joe, it's nice to see you on a miserable day like this.' Really she was very pleased to see him. It cheered up her day no end.

'I've got your message. Mrs. Haines just told me you wanted to see me. What a pity I'm married. She didn't tell me what you wanted me for and I'm not much good at guessing.'

'I had asked Bob Evans to come and do my garden and he

51

said he'd come and do it but he's broken his leg. I expect that you know all about that. Mrs Haines suggested that you might be interested?'

'I'll be pleased to look after it for you. I like gardening,' he told her. 'You tell me what you like and I'll do my best to do it. We'll have to wait until spring.'

'I'm going to make a drink. What would you like, tea or coffee?'

'Coffee I think, Annabel.'

'Come through to the kitchen, Joe.' She knew that he was happier in the kitchen than the sitting room.

While they were having their drink Joe thought that he'd better tell her what was being said.

'Miss Thomas reckons you're undercutting 'er and she's lost quite a bit of trade since you've been 'ere. She's an old skinflint. Some of her loyal supporters were saying unkind things about you which is making bad feeling in the parish.'

'I'm sorry to hear this,' said Annabel.

'Lies can be very dangerous things,' Joe said.

'Take no notice. She's had no competition before and it'll take her off her 'igh 'orse for a bit.'

Annabel had not heard anything directly about the depth of the bad feeling. She knew that there must be some because she was in competition with Miss Thomas but as far as she knew there was nothing sinister in it. It was just business rivalry.

What Miss Thomas didn't like was being taken by surprise. She was not ready or prepared for the competition. Miss Thomas considered that Mrs Neilson had played her a dirty trick.

On the Sunday, Father Patrick O'Hara asked members of the congregation if they would support Father John at Madley Cross where he was going to give six open air sermons starting on the Wednesday next at 2 o'clock. Mrs Walters, sitting in the next seat to Annabel offered to take her.

'I'll pick you up Wednesday afternoon at half past one,' she said.

'I'll get Vera to look after the shop. Vera's very good like that.'

It certainly was a new experience for those who went. It was a real mediaeval affair. The tall figure in a long black cassock and tonsured haircut held forth with great zest. As a backdrop stood the ancient parish church of Madley and in the little square was the post office on the one side, and on the other side a butcher's shop with the owner's name, JACK HEWER, FAMILY BUTCHER, written in bold black letters on an off-white background which was fastened above the shop window.

Round the cross stood a small crowd, some listening and some telling him to go home. Their ignorance and prejudice gave a clear picture of how strong the bad felling was against the Roman Catholics. Their hatred spilled over at Madley Cross.

The big burly policeman was there leaning on his bicycle in case some fanatic started something. The people in Madley didn't like PC Willis from Kingstone. He was too quick with his notebook and pencil.

'You could hardly call it a religious event when the police had to be there to keep order,' said Mrs Walters and Annabel agreed with her.

Some days later, Annabel was talking to a lady, a Mrs Brown from Thruxton.

'I went to hear the preacher at Madley Cross and I could not help my thoughts wandering when I noticed the church in the background. I wonder if I could see over it sometime when it is open.

'I know one of the churchwardens,' Mrs Brown said. 'I'm sure that he'd love to show you round the church. I'll ask Leslie Powell to take us round one evening. He's the vicar's warden and has a church key.'

'Oh, that is kind of you. I'd love that.'

On a beautiful sunny afternoon Mrs Brown called for Annabel and they went to see over Madley parish church dedicated to the Nativity of the Blessed Virgin Mary. As they walked round, Mr Powell pointed out various things.

'There are three graceful arcades dating from 1300. The dark old pulpit is Jacobean. It is a beautiful open and airy church with "lights" in the clerestory. They are not called windows, they are called "lights",' he explained.

Annabel noticed two solid oak pews which didn't look too old and so she mentioned them to Mr Powell.

'These look new,' said Annabel.

'There's a tale about these pews,' Mr Powell said.

'Oh, do tell,' Annabel asked.

'A long time ago two pews were removed. There was no record why but the markings are still there where they stood so the vicar decided to replace them.

'Now there are two cabinetmakers in the parish and the vicar didn't know which one to ask to make the replacement pews. To cut it short he went round to see both craftsmen and asked them to make a small casket five inches long four inches wide and three and a half inches deep and he wanted a hinged lid on top. They both took down the measurements and asked how soon he wanted it. The vicar told one to deliver his casket in a fortnight and he told the other that he'd call by and collect it at the shop as he was passing nearly every day.

'When the two weeks were up, the one who was bringing it to the vicarage came with his casket and the vicar called and collected the other casket. He examined the caskets with great care. There was very little difference that he could find. The lid in one casket fitted just that little bit better than the other. He opened and shut both lids several times before making his decision. These are the pews and they will remain here for centuries to come. Unfortunately this story will be forgotten unless I write it down and place it in the vestry safe.'

'What a lovely story. I expect there are many more, long since forgotten.'

'There are bound to be with a church so old but we will never hear them.'

The fourteenth-century painted glass in the windows

looked beautiful as the shafts of sunlight shone through them. As they left the church they both thanked Leslie for showing them round and making it so interesting.

The following Thursday Annabel was seen riding in Fred White's new car. By Friday midday it was common knowledge that they'd been out together. Fred didn't care how many knew, but Annabel felt that people were jumping to conclusions far too soon. She liked Fred but as yet, at any rate, it was no love match. She enjoyed the meal very much. For one thing, she didn't have to prepare it, which in itself was quite a treat.

Country folk don't miss much. If anything moves in their small world they spot it. They knew that George Lewis called every day for his paper, as did Fred White, and Fred didn't mind people knowing that he was sweet on Annabel.

The priest was also a regular visitor. They all knew that Annabel was a good Roman Catholic. Joe Morgan called always at or after 6 p.m. but he never stayed long. This also was noted.

Rob Sadler brought the eggs, mostly before closing time.

The first time he went to the shop he told Annabel, 'You could sell some of my eggs. If you like I'll bring you four dozen and I'll sell them to you at the wholesale price and you should make a nice bit if people want them.'

It was agreed in a business-like way. He delivered the eggs once a week. He had a reputation as a womanizer but not with Annabel.

There were also some attractive salesmen who called from time to time but, as far as anyone could see, they all came in working hours.

Of course, there were people coming and going all day long and so Annabel's conduct was never in question. The milkman called every day about 8 a.m. and he usually whistled a tune as he ladled out the milk with his pint measure into a jug placed there for the purpose. Then he carefully replaced the cloth over the jug. The beads stopped the wind blowing it away and the cloth protected the contents from the birds. He had his own stories to tell. On one occasion he could not read the note a lady had left for him so he knocked at the door to ask her. The front door was mostly mottled glass because her husband wanted to have more light in the room. She opened the door and put her head round to answer the milkman's knock. She told him that she wanted another pint as she had visitors coming. She hadn't got a stitch on and all could be seen through the mottled glass. she had no idea that she was showing him all her charms.

Mostly the postman had gone by the time the milkman came. He was not as time-conscious as the postman.

Ted Banks, the postman, was a cheerful person. He liked his work and he liked walking, which was just as well as he had long distances to cover. He too knew a great deal about what was happening on his rounds. He would scan the picture postcard and tell the recipient with a smile, 'Your friends are having a lovely holiday, and they are having better weather than us.'

It was rather annoying being told the message which was for the recipient only but there was no harm in him. He was just a bit nosy.

Roger Tomkin's wife, Nancy, who worked at Morris's farm helping Betty Morris in the house, announced in the shop, 'Mrs Morris has just had a little boy. It's their third and she says that it will be the last, if she 'as got anything to do with it.'

Maggie Bowlan, who could not help hearing what was being said, laughingly remarked, 'What's she going to do? 'ave 'im immunized?'

'I expects they'll think of something,' said Nancy Tomkins. 'I see,' she went on, 'Bob Evans is getting used to his plastered leg. Shouldn't be too long before the district nurse will get it off of 'im.'

'He hasn't had such a fuss for a long time,' said Maggie Bowlan. 'He says he won't do such a daft thing again.'

The smell of the new loaves of bread still filled the shop. They looked very appetizing on the shelves behind the counter.

'I rather like this shop bread. I didn't at first,' said Nancy Tomkin to the others in the shop. 'There was a time,' she continued, 'when no one would buy it.' When they looked at her white hair they knew that her memory lane was a long one. 'They were a bit suspicious about what was in it. How things have changed. Now it's commonplace to buy bread. Now only a few people bake their own bread.'

'Things are changing, all the time. Look at the number of motor cars there are today. I expect there'll come a day when every house will have one,' said Maggie Bowlan.

'I think a change is a good thing,' Annabel said.

In the back of her mind was the hope that Pat would change his religion and marry her. Annabel didn't live in a world of faith, hope and make-believe. Pat needed love and marriage, which was natural, and he could have that in a real union, not just a mental one which was cold and physically loveless.

'I'll have to try and reason with him,' she told herself. 'He says he's married to the Church. If that were true, he'd be committing adultery if he makes love with me. Being married to a man-made institution is very different from a personal love relationship, "to have and to hold". Being married is a personal commitment,' she reasoned. 'I can't have a personal relationship with a thing. The church is teaching fossilized mediaeval dictates. They might have been practicable for a past age but they are no use for the present.

'Poor Pat's in chains made by man, not God, and I must try and break them. Perhaps he'll listen to sweet reason. He's such a gentle soul and the church is so masterful. He's terrified of hellfire. I believe,' Annabel thought. 'God is loving and full of compassion and understands better than the church with its hard rules.'

The women in the shop had gone on talking but Annabel was not listening. She came back to earth like awakening out of a dream. She served them one by one and soon the shop was silent again. It had been a pleasant morning and the bad weather hadn't kept them in when they wanted something. The shop was doing well and she was getting regular cus-

57

tomers now who gave her a greater sense of security.

There was a love song in her heart but it was muted by the cold loveless set of rules. She wondered if she could break this love-killing barrier.

'I want him for myself', she said out loud.

She was in love with Pat.

6

Father Patrick was calling regularly twice a week now and their time together went by so quickly. They had fallen in love. Annabel couldn't wait for him to come to her. It was quite dark at half past six and he came different ways so as not to make his calling too noticeable.

It had been a busy day for Annabel in the shop. She had had a lot of customers and several deliveries of goods which had to be stacked away on the various shelves in the storeroom. It was all done before closing time but it had been tiring and Annabel was ready to close the shop door for the night.

She felt strangely excited despite being tired. After a quick snack she ran a bath and the two bath cubes frothed and bubbled, giving off a lovely smell of flowers. After she towelled herself dry she dressed in her best underwear, not knowing why, except by intuition, that 'something' might happen tonight when Patrick came.

After what seemed an age of anticipation she heard the gentle tapping on the door. Her heart leapt and she hurried to the door to let him in. He took her in his arms and kissed her.

Sitting together on the settee they both felt a strange tension which had not been present at their previous meetings and, although neither of them spoke, it came as no surprise when Patrick took her by the hand and led her into the bedroom.

He hugged her and kissed her and she could feel that he was excited as he pressed himself to her and she too was feeling her body preparing to love him. He slowly unbuttoned her dress and gently helped her take it off.

'What beautiful underwear you have,' he said as he slowly removed her slip and bra.

He could not go any further until he had fondled her breasts and held her now protruding nipples in his mouth and caressed them with his tongue.

'Now it is my turn to help you out of your clothes,' she said.

First she removed his jacket, then his collar and shirt. Then she slowly undid his trousers, button by button and pulled them down, and then his briefs. Now she saw his upright manhood for the first time. It was big and strong and she went down on her knees and held him in her hands.

'You have a beautiful body,' she said and then she kissed his throbbing penis and excited him with light strokes of her tongue.

Patrick was moaning with excitement.

'Stop, darling, stop,' he begged.

As he rose from her knees she still held him with one hand and put the other on his warm back and pressed herself to him.

As he enfolded her in his arms he whispered, 'This is beautiful.'

Lifting her on the bed, he took the rest of her clothes off and went down on her and with his tongue soon brought her to her first climax. He caressed her whole body and with his tongue brought her to the point of no return again.

It had been a long time since she had had the thrill of making love. The excitement was so intense that she had multiple waves of passion. It was an experience out of this world. Pat's feeling of guilt was swept away. The mighty wave of passion had engulfed his whole being.

'I do not feel guilty, neither must you. It's the most natural thing that could happen. I have never experienced love with someone who loves me and wants me.'

'I'm the same, darling, I have an overwhelming desire to give myself to you, to be possessed, to be held in a rapturous embrace. I am ready to take all of you.'

'I want you inside,' she said and with her soft hand she guided him into her inviting body and felt that it was the fulfilling of a wonderful dream. During the slow thrusting rhythm they both reached a glorious climax. It was the most exciting experience of their lives. Annabel had never known that loving could be so exciting. They both had had past experiences but somehow this was *completely* satisfying. It was to be the first of many loving evenings together.

When they had had some supper, they held each other again. Not a word was spoken. The silence carried their thoughts. She put her hand on him and he cupped her warm soft breast in his hand and they both became excited again but he told her that he would have to go. As it was, he'd have to make excuses for being late if he were asked. As he left he heard voices being carried on the wind. Men were coming down one of the three roads. Father Patrick took one of the other roads so as not to be seen. The stars seemed to dance between the hurrying clouds. He had known it darker many a time.

He quickly moved away from the voices and the wind helped to muffle any sound he made. He'd have to say that he had been dealing with a marriage problem, that should cover his lateness.

He said to himself, 'I'll have to leave earlier next time.'

His dark suit helped to hide him from the poacher's keen eye. But he was getting more concerned about getting into the abbey without causing questions to be thought, let alone asked.

As he made his way back to the abbey in the silence of the night, he thought a great deal about his relationship with Annabel. Only now, when he was alone with the stars and away from the influence of Annabel, could he reason things clearly in a different way – the way the Church thought. He knew that these things happened and sometimes it had caused a great deal of upset. Annabel to him was like a strong magnet whose influence he could not resist. The joy and the excitement, he considered were worth the risk. Yet it worried him. He'd have to get away to break the temptation.

He remembered being told, when he was training for the priesthood, 'There are some temptations too strong to stop by an act of will. The only way out of the trap, especially a sex trap, is to run like hell to get away from the consuming fire of desire.'

Move right away. The young priests were advised to move to another part of the country or even another country. There were always openings in the mission field. that was the only way the grip of the temptation could be broken.

Annabel silently shut the door by holding the bell so that it would not ring and attract attention. It was very late. She wanted to get the light out so as not to let the late people know she was still up.

She never thought that love would come her way again, especially in the fullness she was experiencing. She could hardly wait for him to come again. Even his voice excited her, not to mention his strong lean body.

It was when they were in a loving embrace that she had said, 'I'd love you to be with me always so that we could love each other and look after one another. No more frustrations and emptiness and bitter loneliness, which we both have experienced for long enough. It is time to start again. That is the solution. But it'd mean that you'd have to leave the Church.'

Annabel had little idea what she was asking Patrick O'Hara to do. He was a deeply superstitious man. He believed in the little people. If anyone queried his belief in these matters they would see the blood coming up his neck and he'd get very angry.

He had watched the will-o-the-wisp dance over the bogs on his home farm. They were the lights of the little people. As a child he had listened to the old folklore tales of magic, of Irish saints travelling to Iceland and pagan heroes seeking lands beyond the sunset. He had listened to tales of fairies who could find hidden treasures invisible to mortals. All this superstition was mixed with angels and blessings and curses. He had absorbed all the mythology and the theology like two blobs of ink and himself like blotting paper. He had absorbed the lot as one consensus of belief. He believed in the works good and bad of the little people as he believed in the Saints Peter and Paul and all the other saints. He had been taught that there was only one church, it was the gate to heaven and there was no other, not to mention what he had understood as hell which had to be avoided at all costs. This meant that he dare not leave the Church and marry Annabel because he was already married to the Church and he would be breaking his vow of chastity. Such an act would be stepping off the path to heaven and slipping straight into the jaws of hell.

How much she wanted him to leave the Church and marry her! Little did she realize what she was wishing from his point of view. If she had known Patrick's hidden self she would have understood why he was quite content to leave this alone. What she'd asked of him he daren't do. He'd burn in hell for all eternity. A touch of sadness came into his thoughts. He didn't want to lose her. Often he felt angry. He was trapped. He sometimes felt angry with God for giving him the facility to make love and then denying him the right to use it.

The following morning Annabel had a pleasant surprise. Vera called.

'I thought you'd like to see Margaret,' she said. She took the shawl away from the tiny face all pink and fresh with blue eyes and red hair like her father.

'She's got Ben's colouring,' Annabel said as she took her in her arms. 'It reminds me of when I held Paul in my arms like this. It only seems like yesterday.' The baby smiled at Annabel and waved her tiny hand about.

'Oh, she's beautiful. You can leave her with me if you like,' Annabel said as she handed her back. It seemed only the other day that Vera had said that she was pregnant. Memories came flooding back of the wedding and how sweet her sisters looked as bridesmaids. She remembered the sunny day and the lovely service.

'Somehow,' Vera said, 'the Church turned making love

into something holy. Married love was blessed in the wedding service. God wants us to enjoy ourselves and the Church rightly blesses the physical union.'

Annabel never thought that Vera would think of the marriage service that way. It was a holy union and that's what she'd like with Patrick, not this secret way of loving.

The grain harvest had been gathered in and most churches had sung their harvest home. Tom Jones, Walter Smith and Evan Williams met for a meeting at the Bowling Green farm.

'I've asked you two to come here to discuss what we can do about ridding our fields of poachers. In a way they do a good job in helping to keep the rabbit population down, while on the other hand our workers are being done out of what they consider a perk and they feel that we are doing nothing to protect their interests.'

'What the hell can we do?'

'We can catch them,' said Tom.

'If we knew how we would've done it years ago.'

'I'm going to suggest to you a way that it can be done,' said Tom. 'That's why I asked you to come tonight.

'Now, in the first place, we have our own men who feel they are being done out. They can help by keeping their ears open and listen to Morgan and the Turner boys in case they let anything drop.'

'That's hardly likely,' said Walter Smith. 'They are a bit too clever for that.'

'We'll have to be as clever as they are.'

'Our lads will be quite willing to help if they know what's going on and they're told what to do, especially when we tell them that they're taking what rightly belongs to them as perks with the job. They must try and find out where they're going to poach next.'

'They always go to the pub at weekends and that is as good a place as anywhere to get close enough to hear if they drop any hints,' said Tom.

They agreed that's what they'd do for the first step and just hope that it worked.

'It's a long shot, but it's worth a try,' Tom said.

Two weeks passed and they had found nothing. Then a week later, on the Friday night, Fred Turner had had too much to drink and the information they had been waiting for came out.

Two of the farmer's sons, Eric Jones and Phil Smith, edged their way near to the Turner boys and Eric said, 'There's not so many rabbits as last year.'

Fred took the bait. He heard that and butted in.

'There be plenty of rabbits about, least-ways there are plenty in Evan Williams's top field with dozens of burrers.'

'Which field be that one then?' Phil Smith asked in a subdued voice.

'The one which 'ad the wheat on it this year.'

'Oh, that 'un.'

'Yes, there be plenty up there but it wona be for long.'

That was the information they'd been waiting for.

'We'll keep watch in relays until they do it.' said Tom.

Evan Williams was just about ready to give up after ten nights when the poachers moved. The local policeman from Kingstone had been told about the plan and they would ring him the minute they started and they'd hold the poachers until he came and booked them. It would be a feather in the policeman's cap if they were caught red-handed. The workmen from the three farms were ready for a call at any moment.

The Turner boys started laying their nets at one thirty on the Sunday morning and the message went out for the men to surround the field. Joe Morgan was on the other side of the field, holding the excited dogs, waiting for the signal to let them go.

Once the dogs started to run, the poachers' eyes were on the rabbits until flash lights shone all round the field and the poachers were caught, all of them, and PC Willis took their names and addresses. This was not like last time, when they only caught one of them.

It was Joe Morgan who had been caught before but this time it was well-planned and they were all netted: the poachers, dogs, rabbits and gear.

The poachers were taken to court and the magistrate did not deal lightly with Joe Morgan. All his equipment was confiscated and his two dogs were to be put down and he was fined £200. A gasp was heard in the courtroom. He had been found out in the act and he had no excuse. All he could do was to plead guilty. The magistrate was much more lenient with the Turner lads whom he considered had been led astray by the older man. He fined Fred £25, Tom £20 and he told them that he would not be so kind to them a second time.

'Next time you come before this bench, Joe Morgan, on a similar charge I shall not hesitate to send you to gaol.'

The court case was the talk of the parish for some time.

Annabel was very sad at the news, she loved Joe, in a strange kind of way. It was more than a physical appeal, that was only a part of his charm. He was a personification of the country but Annabel saw Joe as part of it and she loved him in it. He knew so much about the country: the animals like the stoat and the weasel, rabbits and foxes; the trees and the inhabitants of the hedgerow. He could also tell what the weather was going to be by looking at the clouds.

Fred Turner was blamed by Joe and Tom for being drunk and opening his mouth. By and large, the people thought that they deserved their punishment and approved the sentences.

Jack Davies was out ploughing, getting the ground ready for the winter sowing and the other workmen were hedging and ditching. The days were drawing in again and mists hung on the landscape but it was nevertheless quite pleasant for November. There were still some rabbits about and quite a few pheasants and soon it would be swede raising time. There was always something happening.

It's a good time to lift the swedes after the frost, but it's a very cold job for the bare hands. The long evenings had come but now the electric light had come to Clehonger and so they could read or play cards in the bright light.

Still some autumn leaves clung to the trees, giving the last bit of colour before the hard winter came. It was like a beautiful sunset before the dark night. The last of the roses were still in full bloom but the bird-song had practically gone and so had the house martins and the swifts.

'Our two fine song birds, the blackbird and the thrush are still with us,' said Jack, the ploughman. 'The birds' best bet for a meal now is with me behind the plough. There's always a fat worm pushed to the surface by the plough. The seagulls know where to find a good feed.'

The winter time was John Taylor's busy time. He had got a new load of elm timber in. He reckoned that elm made good coffins. He knew that the cold winds sorted the old people out. It's a job to keep warm both in the farm house and the cottage. There was enough wind coming under the doors to blow a ship along. The old found being in bed was the warmest place but they couldn't stay in bed all winter. Dr Foster tried to save them. If he failed, John Taylor and the vicar did the last acts for them.

When the snow came, that really was the worst time. The narrow lanes filled up with snow which was blown off the fields into the cuttings. Sometimes villages were cut off for days.

George Lewis was always glad when winter was over. The cold weather had helped to sell his beautiful warm, well-lined slippers. But he'd never seen the beauty of the hoarfrost on the trees and hedgerows.

As George discovered, even the country folk, who are used to these sights, still stop and admire the white wonder which surrounds them. Joe Morgan told George about the hundreds and hundreds of spiders he'd see in the hedgerow on a hoarfrost morning.

'You don't actually see them.' he said, 'but you see all the hundreds of webs they have made when they are covered with hoar frost.' George had never seen anything like it in his life. He was really enjoying living in the country. He met a chap, Eddie Mason in The Plough.

Over a pint Eddie said.

'I'm going back to Brum. We can't stick another winter

here. We miss the shops and the street lighting and the gas for cooking.'

'How do you like it?' Eddie asked George.

'I'm getting used to it. I think the air is better for my chest so I'm staying. Winter isn't all that long.'

Father Patrick was also on the move. He could see the jaws of hell yawning before him if he continued his association with Annabel. He too had made a decision to move away from Clehonger, so he'd applied to go back to Ireland because his mother was not at all well. He felt that he had to get away from this compelling temptation.

Father Patrick had been thinking all day how he was going to break the news to Annabel that he was going back to Ireland. He thought it best to spread the blame and put himself in the 'sympathy bracket'.

It was a cold night so Annabel offered Pat a whisky. For a while they talked small talk as they sat in each other's arms. The whisky was giving him courage to tell her.

'Annabel, darling,' he started, 'I've some bad news I'm afraid.'

Annabel looked at him as the colour drained from her face.

'I've had a letter from my dad telling me that my mother is ill. She is asking for me. I told the abbot and he said I could go and see my sick mother and stay awhile until she gets better. "If need be," the abbot said, "I'll find a new opening over there for you." I told him that I was grateful for his concern and that there was no need for me to stay in Ireland.'

'You refused a new post didn't you, darling?'

'It's not as easy as that, my love. When the abbot says, I have found you another post, he means you are being sent, you have no option, but I did try. He did say that he'd be glad to have me back in my parish here if I'm not away too long. I've got a feeling that the abbot knows something about us. He didn't mention anything but we all know the form. If he thinks we are being tempted to leave the Church because of a

68

woman, the usual thing is to remove the priest at short notice. This is short notice and so someone could have said something.'

'Patrick, darling, leave this terrible heartless Church. Let us get married. I have business here and the parish is expanding and soon, very soon, the shop will support both of us.'

'Annabel, darling, I am thinking about it all the time.

Annabel burst into tears and flung her arms round his neck.

'I love you, dearest. If I've got to give you up or the Church I'd give up the Church. If you love me you'll do the same.'

'I'm not a layman, darling. I can't act on the spur of the moment. I've got to think. You must be patient. I'm married to the Church. I am committed.

'I'll do what I have to do. The Church is very hard on those who break their vows.'

He held her in his arms and she cried.

'If you love me so much why don't you rebel and leave this cruel mind-bending regime?'

'I'll have to go, my dearest Annabel. It's no good. I feel I'm being watched all the time.'

Annabel dried her eyes. They were red with crying.

'Leave this inhuman mental prison and marry me, darling. We are meant for each other.

'I'll do what I can. I love you, darling.'

He left her with tears in his eyes knowing there was no chance of changing anything but it softened the blow for Annabel. He'd put the blame for his move on the Church and he'd left her with a glimmer of hope which he knew didn't exist.

Even the bleak winter had its happy moments for the country people. Not only was it hedging and ditching time it was also pig killing time.

'It is surprising how far a pig's squeal can be heard when it is being killed,' Tom Povey remarked. He had come from Wolverhampton. He liked the country and was beginning to notice things. He stood and watched the four men using all their strength to hold the fifteen score pig on a bench while the fifth man used a stunning gun, which made the pig unconscious, then he killed it with a long-bladed knife. Nothing was lost – even the blood was caught in a bucket. When it was dead they put it on a large heap of straw and burnt the pig's hairs off. Then it was washed and scraped clean before being cut in pieces.

Later on that night, faggots were made and pork pies were baked and sausages and brawn were prepared. All the farmers' wives worked very hard. Then the menfolk came and they all sat down to a grand meal at about two thirty in the morning. They had roast pork and all the trimmings.

Annabel was invited to one of these affairs and watched the girls work. She really enjoyed her night. It did her good to put her other worries aside for an hour or so. As she was leaving a parcel was thrust into her hands and when she got home she had a look at what she had been given. There was a piece of liver, two faggots, sausages and little bits of trimmings called 'fry'. She enjoyed two good meals the next day. If she ate like the farmers wives she'd soon have to have new clothes.

It was always a solemn and happy time when the pig was killed. It was sad because the pig was treated as a pet and fed with loving care and yet it was a joyful time because all the good bacon and ham would be enjoyed in the coming months.

Vera came into the shop one cold morning and said, 'Have you heard the news? Father Patrick is leaving to go to Ireland.' The thought of Pat leaving made her feel sick. She held tight to the counter, but nothing of the pain showed on her face. She had pressed him hard to leave the Church and marry her but he said he couldn't do that. Annabel found it hard to understand. The situation between them had become very difficult.

Surely he would come and explain. She waited that evening and the next but he didn't come. The shock had now turned to anger that he could treat her like this. Had his loving been for his own selfish gratification. She had given her all when she gave herself to him and he had thrown it back at her. She had been humiliated to the point of fury. He had left without even saying goodbye.

It was in the winter months that a whist drive and dance went down well. However wet or cold it was, there was always a good turn out. Dick Ridler, the owner of the cider works had a dance for his workforce and, of course, others came and joined in the fun. Very few knew how kind-hearted and helpful he was to those in need. His dance in the works was the big event of the year.

Annabel had been invited but she didn't want to go. She was not in the mood. She was angry and disappointed. She had to face it and not give the villagers an inkling of her feelings. One lady did remark that she was looking pale but Annabel laughed it off and said she had a few late nights stocktaking in preparation for Christmas.

Patrick had gone out of her life and the loss was as great as when she lost Henry but this time her grief had to be born in secret.

There was plenty of cider to drink, but Annabel dare not drink much of it.

'It's dangerous stuff unless you're used to it,' she was told. There was plenty of food but she only pretended she was enjoying the sandwiches and cakes.

The young and old had an enjoyable evening. A good time was had round the sheds too as time was to prove, with more weddings and baptisms.

Annabel would have loved to have danced with Patrick but, of course, he was not there. Joe was there and he danced with her and she soon discovered how he felt towards her as he held her tightly to himself, but for her it was 'no'. He was married.

Several of the men danced with her but she saved the last dance for Joe and she told him how sorry she was he'd been caught.

'Never mind it was good fun while it lasted,' he said. He

71

had brushed it off. 'In any case it's not worth going to prison for, so that's the end of the line for me, I'll stick to my rat-catching in future.'

'That Joe, she said, 'is a wise decision.'

Joe walked her home. He put his arm round her but they didn't stop until they reached her gate. He took her in his arms but little did he know how vulnerable she was because of Pat's decision to leave her. He kissed her for the first time and she lovingly responded.

'I've wanted to do this for a long time,' he told her.

'Yes, Joe, I've known that for a long time. Oh, if only you were single.'

How easily they could have made love. She knew how he was feeling and her feelings were the same as his. She gave him a big kiss. She tried to get away but he held her in his strong arms. As he slackened his grip she gave him a loving tender kiss and ran to the house. As she was shutting the door she waved him a kiss and was gone.

He still could hear her words.

'If only you were single.'

7

Annabel was thinking about Joe as she got into bed and she knew that she was courting temptation. She was still having a tearful time over Pat and she knew that Joe could bring her much comfort. She was longing for the forbidden fruit a relationship could offer. She was in the same position with Joe as Pat was with her. Her relationship with Pat had jelled but she was forbidden fruit for Pat.

There was no such difficulty with Fred. On the surface Annabel and Fred would enjoy a happy marriage. Fred had no impedimenta like Pat and Joe. He was young and ambitious and he was on the threshold of entering a new and fascinating motor car sales and service business.

The three times they went out the main topic of conversation had been about the business. Annabel could see that she'd be the wife of a motor car fanatic. She could see herself becoming another kind of widow. On this third occasion she thought it best to say what she had been thinking.

As she lay in her warm bed she lived again her talk with Fred.

'I'm sure, dear, I could grow to love you very much but I feel for your happiness. You need not only someone younger than me but also younger than you.'

'After Paul was born the doctor told me that I could not have another child. Henry and I were very upset about this but we had the one which gave us great joy. I don't think, Fred, that I'm the one for you. The next few years will be very hectic. You'll need a young wife to help carry the tensions and stresses you'll have to face.'

She remembered him saying, 'I could manage these things better if you were by my side, darling.'

Perhaps I was a bit hard, she thought, when she said, 'Yes, darling, but women grow older faster than men. There are always attractive and ambitious young women ready to take my place who could give you children, if that's what you want.'

'I haven't given it a lot of thought. You're way ahead of me in your thinking,' Fred had replied.

'That's because I'm older than you. I want you to be happy. But with me there are too many unsolvable problems to spell lasting happiness.

'We must be honest with ourselves. Soon you'd be looking upon me as a mother and looking somewhere else for a lover.'

'I suppose you are right, dear,' Fred replied, 'but I want to be a close friend.'

Annabel still hoped that Patrick would find a way and come back to her. Life was sad and empty without him. She turned over and soon sleep took charge of all her problems.

Ernie Martin was also finding life sad and empty. He had been a keen fisherman nearly all his life. One of his greatest joys was to get away from Birmingham one day in the week and go fishing. He had worked in the BSA motor-cycle works. If he took a day off in the week he worked Sundays on double time which meant that he had his day off for free.

He used to go to Ironbridge and fish in the River Severn from the wharfage. He liked to fish even if he caught nothing but he rarely came home empty-handed.

Mabel, his wife, had died just under a year before and he had tried to manage on his own but he didn't take much persuading by his daughter, Annie, to come and live with them in Clehonger. Bill Watts, her husband, was a motor mechanic and he had moved out of Birmingham on doctor's orders three years previously and his chest was a lot better now that he was out of the polluted air. He now worked at Lloyd and Williams' garage in Hereford.

Ernie was going deaf but he would not admit it.

He said, 'People don't speak proper otherwise I'd be able to 'ear 'um.'

When Ernie came back from The Plough he seemed so happy and cheerful that Annie wondered what he'd been drinking.

'What 'ave you been drinking, Dad?'

He laughed and said, 'Nothing special.'

'I met a bloke called Tom Macklin in the pub and we got talking about fishing. He offered to show me where he goes fishing tomorrow morning. 'You come with me tomorrow morning and I'll take you to where I go,' he said. I thanked 'im. It's bottom fishing mind, Tom warned me, but that's better 'an no fishing at all.

'I'm going to meet him outside the pub in the morning at 7.30.'

It did not seem to be a hardship for Annie. Breakfast was always at 7.00 as Bill had to be at work by 8.00.

'I'll go and collect my gear for morning then.'

'Breakfast as usual then, dad?'

'That's fine.'

Ten minutes later he returned with what he thought would be all he needed for his outing. Annie could not help seeing how happy he looked. No one knew how much he missed his fishing. She thought, as she gave him his breakfast of two eggs and bacon, how bright he seemed. She had never realized how much it meant to him.

'The fog's lifting,' Annie remarked. 'It must have been bad in the night. Mind you wrap up well. We don't want any bad chests and running noses.'

'Don't you start fussing. Your mother did enough of that.'

As Bill, her husband, was putting his coat on, Annie warned her Bill to be careful with all this fog about.

'You've got plenty of time. Another cup of tea, Dad?'

'No thank you dear. I must be getting off too. I don't like holding people up.'

'It's only a quarter past seven, Dad. You don't want to be standing about in the cold.' Ernie kept his eye on the grandfather clock.

75

At twenty past seven he put his heavy coat on saying as he did so, 'Well, I'll be off then. I'll be back about 8.30 a.m.'

As he went out Annie shouted at him, 'Be careful now. See you later.'

He was so happy that he didn't mind the fog and the cold. Tom, his new friend, was already there so there was no waiting about. His car had seen better days but it was better than walking. It was very quiet. There was not a soul about.

On their way down Tom told him all about Clehonger pool.

'First of all there is a spring at the bottom and so the pool is always full. No one knows how deep it is. Really, it's a small lake and the water is always fresh and clear.

'It's quite a feature of the parish, if for nothing else, for the amount of birds it attracts every year.'

'I used to know a bit about birds,' said Ernie. 'Which ones come 'ere?'

'I'll tell yer if I can remember 'um all. First there be the 'ouse martins, they come 'ere about April. They come by the 'undreds, I nearly said thousands. It seems like that. They build their nests of mud and straw under the eaves all round the school which is just over the way. Then there's the swifts. I reckon they are the fastest birds on earth. They come because of the pool. They have their nests in the church eaves. They screech round the church tower at fantastic speeds catching flies and they skim over the water at the same speed, catching flies or drinking water. Did you know they can't land on the ground?'

'No,' said Ernie.

'If they fall to the ground they cannot take off again, their little legs are too short. Many a time I've found them and tossed them up in the air and they fly off at high speed,' Tom said with a laugh. 'Would you believe it, a pair of swans come every year, rear their young and fly off in the autumn.'

'I like swans. They are so graceful,' said Ernie.

'There are at least two pairs of moorhens which have made the pool their permanent home. The pool is alive with tiny frogs in the spring time, and it is difficult not to walk on them.'

'A bloke said to me, "I wouldn't leave Birmingham and bury myself in the country,"' said Ernie. 'There is more going on than you think, I told him. It looks quiet enough but really it's buzzing with life.'

' 'Ave you lived here a long time?' asked Ernie.

'Yes,' said Tom, 'all me life.'

'By the way, if you like walking there is a short cut from 'ere to 'Ereferd.' He was reminded when he saw a man coming from the Hereford direction across the field they were in. The path went past the pool where they were standing.

'It cuts off about a mile and a 'alf. You see that road up there?' asked Tom, pointing to it.

'Oh, yes, I see it now.'

'That's called the back road to Eaton Bishop. This path crosses that road and continues along the bank of the river Wye to Wye bridge in 'Ereferd. It's practically a straight path all the way. You can come back on the bus.'

It was now 8.15 a.m. and they decided to pack up. They had not caught anything but they had each enjoyed the other's company. 'If we were walking now,' Tom was telling Ernie, 'we'd pass the church and continue across three fields to the Bowling Green Farm and down the pitch and along Gosmore Lane.' Tom was glad he'd kept the car, he couldn't do the walking like he used to do.

When they reached William's corner they joined a small crowd and Annie, Ernie's daughter, was among them.

Ted Banks, the postman was telling his story of how he found Mrs Neilson's dead body.

Annie came across to her dad and got hold of his arm.

'What's 'e say? Murder! Who?', he asked in a loud voice.

'Be quiet, Dad. I'll tell you after'.

'Who has been murdered?' He asked again in a loud voice.

'Mrs Neilson.'

'Where?'

'At the shop. Now be quiet and I will tell you later, but let me listen.'

Ted Banks, the postman, was repeating himself because Ernie's loud voice had upset his flow.

77

'As I was saying, I got to 'er place about 7.30 a.m. and the shop door was open. I shouted "post" but there was no reply so I puts my 'ead round the door and shouts again. I thought she was in the kitchen. I peeped in, but I couldn't see nothing. Then, as my eyes got used to the bad light, I thought I saw a foot with a slipper on it at the end of the counter. I hurried to the end of the counter and there she was in a pool of blood in 'er nightie which was ripped to shreds, and her face was all covered in blood. Her poor legs all covered in dark red bruises and the same with her arms. 'Er nightie 'ad been ripped and her breast that was showing was covered in blood. She must 'ave put up a terrific fight. I've never seen such a horrible sight.

'What she die of, Ted? Was she stabbed?'

'I don't know 'ow she died but with all that blood about she could have been stabbed.'

There was dead silence while that sank in and so he went on.

'I stood there stunned for a minute, or perhaps it were two minutes, then I realized that I was badly shaken.

'Then I remembered that I must report it to the police. I found the telephone book but I was shaking so bad it took me a time to find his number. I quite forgot to dial 999, I was in such a fluster.

'Eric Willis was 'aving his breakfast when I rang and he answered the phone and told me to stay with the body until he came and not to let nobody in before 'e got 'ere. He was in a real sweat when 'e arrived. He'd cycled the three and a half miles from Kingston in double quick time. He was soaking wet with sweat in those heavy clothes of 'is. 'E 'ad to 'ave a look first.

''E asked me, "Ave you touched anythin?" which I 'adn't. I told 'im only the telephone to ring 'yer.'

'That's good,' 'e says, 'Now I 'ave to take your statement.'

'I asked 'im what he meant?'

'You got to tell me what 'appened and I've got to write it down and out came 'is notebook but he 'adn't got a pencil, 'e'd left it be'ind in 'is 'urry. He had to borrow mine. 'E was still breathing 'ard and 'e were painfully slow writing down what I told 'im word for word. Then 'e made me sign it before he'd let me go. I never wants to see the likes of that again.'

'So it weren't an accident then, Ted?'

'No, it looked like a terrible murder to me. I must get on with my letters now. Ta-ta.'

Little groups wandered off in twos and threes. Gorsty Common was in shock. Death was bad enough but for an attractive woman to be struck down in her prime was unbelievable.

Inspector Trevor Powell and his assistant, Sergeant Leslie Smith of the CID, were not trained in country ways, neither did they understand the minds of the villagers.

Neither did the villagers know that Inspector Powell had always been a stickler for detail. Trevor had a tidy mind. He couldn't live in a state of confusion.

He believed, as he told his Sergeant, 'Look at the details and they will lead you to the answer you are seeking.'

A knife was missing. It worried him and angered him when he couldn't find the knife which belonged to the set. It was very likely to be the same knife which was used to kill the victim. He would take the place to pieces to find it if need be.

Sergeant Leslie Smith could grasp a situation. He saw the whole picture. He made notes of his findings and thoughts for future reference. He also, in another book, took notes for his boss. As a policeman he took a general view while the inspector, as an artist in investigation, took particular interest in the little things which made up the whole, like the Victorian illustrators who took great care over the details which made the picture much more interesting. A mountain lake was one thing but put a man fishing on the lake and the whole picture comes to life.

The inspector worked from the detail to the whole crime and the sergeant worked from the crime to the details.

These two men suited each other and worked as an excellent team. They often irritated each other with their

79

stance but their thinking was complementary.

Their first big task was to try to understand the minds of the local people. The murder was, in comparison, a straightfoward procedure but to break down the suspicion of 'foreigners' trampling over their private lives and to try and tear apart their loyalty to each other in the parish was quite another thing.

The inspector was to learn that when trouble comes the local people cling together as a form of protection. It becomes a tight community and it is difficult to break the barrier down. People who had come to live in the place twenty or more years ago were still considered foreigners and looked upon with suspicion. It was with some trepidation that Powell viewed the task before him.

The local policeman had called the superintendent who told him to stay put until Inspector Powell arrived. It took the inspector long enough to come, he thought. It was nearly half past ten when he arrived. A host of others had also come. PC Eric Willis had been standing round like an out of date law book.

The voice of the law had said, 'Now, Willis, you must stay there and make sure that no one gets in near the body until Inspector Powell comes. Have you got that?'

'Yes, sir.'

Now the place was flooded out with officialdom: several policeman of various ranks, police photographers, fingerprint men and the police doctor who pronounced Annabel Neilson dead and gave the time of her death as somewhere between 11.00 p.m and 3.00 a.m.

The whole group came under the heading The Murder Squad. It might have been a shock for the postman and for the local policeman who tried to give the impression that he was used to such things as murder.

'Oh, you get used to these things in the police.' he said. 'But I must admit that I was shaken when I saw the state of the body. I could tell she had put up a brave fight, poor woman.'

Quite apart from the official people, the press were there. Not just the local papers were represented but the national papers had sent their representatives to get the story. They did not stay at the scene. When they had got what they could out of the police they were off round Gorsty Common and picked up little pieces of information like pieces of a jigsaw puzzle.

'How did she get on with Miss Thomas? Was there any rivalry?'

Those who were asked tried to be noncommittal but with skillful questioning the reporters got what they were after.

'Could Miss Thomas cope with the extra work since more people have come into the place?'

'Oh yes, she could. Actually, things had gone a bit slack since the other shop had opened.'

'You mean that Mrs Neilson was doing better at her expense?'

'No, I wouldn't say that.'

'But that's what you meant.'

'Yes I suppose so. She wasn't doing badly. She had her regular customers. But to be honest, she'd lost a few of her customers because of her prices.'

'Wasn't it said that Mrs Neilson was undercutting Miss Thomas to capture her trade? Wasn't that true? Someone said that's what was happening.'

'It did look like that, I must admit.'

'So you would say there was bad feeling between them?'

'I'm not answering any more of your questions. You are trying to catch me out. Good day.'

A lady reporter for a national paper asked Mrs Bowlan with such a sweet smile, 'Do you remember the Trevor Roberts case and the footpath he ploughed up?'

'Oh yes,' said Mrs. Bowlan.

'Do you remember what happened, exactly?'

'There was a pathway across one of 'is fields which was part of a short cut to the village school. The kids used it every day and the parents used it when they had a dance or a whist drive there. This path is used every day or nearly every day of the year. Farmer Roberts went and ploughed it up. The people complained to 'im but he told um where they could go.

'So with the 'elp of Mrs Neilson we got a petition up and the list was on 'er counter and as Mrs Neilson was artic ... What's the word? She could speak well.'

'You mean articulate?'

'Yes, that's the word. We all agreed she should take the petition to Farmer Roberts on our be'alf. He threatened to put the dog on 'er if she didn't get off 'is land.'

'You don't think Mr Roberts had much time for Mrs Neilson.'

'I didn't say that. I don't think 'e 'as much time for any of us. So we went to see Mr Sadler and Mr Taylor and they got a solicitor and we took 'im to court. And he had to put the path back again.'

'So you would say, Mrs Bowlan ... it is Mrs Bowlan isn't it?'

'Yes, that's right.'

'So you would agree that Mrs Neilson had made some enemies?'

'Not that bad to kill 'er.'

'Thank you, Mrs Bowlan.'

'Excuse me, miss, you didn't say which paper you represented, I might like to get a copy tomorrow.'

'It's *The Daily Recorder.*'

'Thank you, miss.'

George Lewis had come to collect his paper. He'd been standing listening to the postman's tale and was very upset.

He said to Ted Banks, 'I hope they get the bastard.'

'I 'ope so too,' said Eric Willis, the policeman. Poor old Ted was badly shaken. Ted Banks continued. 'She were very kind to me,' he said. 'If she were up when I called ... sometimes a bit later than today ... she would give me a cup of tea. She won't give me one no more, poor soul.'

Sergeant had made a list of their findings for the day as follows:

According to the doctor she was murdered between 11.00 p.m. and 3.00 a.m.

The front door of the house and shop had not been

forced. She must have let the person in. It could mean that the person was known to her.

It was late when she had gone to bed.

They had had a cup of tea together. Obviously Annabel looked on the person as a friend.

It was an unexpected caller, otherwise she wouldn't have gone to bed.

She was stabbed and the doctor had said that she had bled to death.

The doctor was uncertain about the knife. A knife was missing from the set of six but the doctor thought the wound was bigger than a knife wound.

There were no incriminating fingerprints. Everything he or she had touched, which included one cup and saucer and the teaspoon, had been wiped. Annabel's fingerprints were still on her cup. The murderer had kept a very cool head to leave no clues before he left the building.

Inspector Powell was reasonably satisfied with the day's work. He was angry at not having found the knife. Now it was the end of a very busy and important day for the local policeman. Inspector and Sergeant Smith were still talking. Willis said to himself, 'I wish they'd go home.'

At last they decided to go. They wished Willis good night as they left the chalet.

When they had gone he said out loud to the empty building, 'I shall be glad to get my feet up.'

The thickening mist swallowed up the police car as it went on its way to Hereford. Willis was glad to be on his way home on his reinforced bicycle. The appealing warmth and love of home urged him on. Even the three miles on a bicycle was a long way after a very trying day. It was freezing now and soon the mist would cover everything with the white lace of hoar frost by morning.

8

George met Joe Morgan in the post office. Olive Taylor had made arrangements with the wholesalers to sell newspapers the same day Mrs Neilson was discovered murdered. On this Tuesday morning she had a great display of daily papers which carried the murder story. Some accounts were more graphic than others.

'I'd like to catch the bugger who did this, George,' Joe said.

'She was a lovely girl. Everyone who knew her said the same thing,' George said.

'I could have gone for her in a big way if my circumstances had been different,' said Joe Morgan.

'I expect there are several men who could say the same thing, including me,' said George.

'I feel sorry for poor old Eric Willis, he's been reduced to a traffic cop. He's been pushed aside by all these big boys from Hereford. I have some idea what he must be feeling. I was in the Birmingham police force for many years.'

'I didn't know that, George. You're a dark horse.'

'I've been out of it for many years. The methods of working have changed a lot since those days,' George replied. 'The basics are the same but their methods are more scientific today.'

'Let's hope their new methods don't let him escape,' said Joe with irony in his voice. 'It wouldn't be the first time that's 'appened!'

'The Murder Squad blokes are hardened investigators. They are not shocked by the sights they see. Murder is murder however it's done. Like the inspector, they seek answers to how, when and why. Each member of the squad is an expert in his field and in time they find the answers and more often than not they catch their murderers.'

'To me,' said Joe they are like ferrets, silent and deadly and efficient, catching their quarry.'

'They'll get him in the end ... I hope,' George concluded.

The inspector and his sergeant looked around the murder scene again. Certain facts were coming to light and every now and then Powell told the Sergeant, 'Make a note of that.'

They had passed from the shop to the kitchen and vice versa several times. Sergeant Smith picked up an article of clothing not far from where the body was found.

'It looks like her dressing gown.' said the inspector.

'Yes it is, sir. It looks as if it has been ripped off but there's no blood on it.' One sleeve had nearly been torn off.

'It looks like she was trying to get away from her attacker but it wasn't to be,' said Powell.

'That means,' said the inspector, 'that she must have known the person.' This fact was substantiated by the two empty tea cups on the table, together with the sugar and milk.

'The person was more than a customer, because they were in the private part of the house and had sat down and had a cup of tea together,' said the inspector.

'Nothing seems to have been stolen,' replied the sergeant. 'No drawers have been opened and the money in the till seemed untouched. That leads us to believe that theft was not the motive.'

'The man could've tried unsuccessfully to rape her. She was covered with bruises on her body and legs. She had obviously fought hard.'

'Yes, that is obvious,' said Leslie Smith. 'I'll bet he had some blood on him, hers and maybe some of his own.'

'One final thing which is of great importance,' Powell remarked. 'The killer had enough cunning to wipe everything clean that had been handled, including the door.'

'I think we are dealing with a person who has brains. He had left nothing in the way of a lead, and the murder weapon had vanished.'

Two more policemen had been sent to do a thorough search. It was a fruitless task. The knife was not in the house or outside the building. More policemen were drafted in to search further afield. Now the road was closed and the whole area was cordoned off so as to make sure that nothing was disturbed. They even searched the road and ditches both sides of the house and then the fields where it could have been thrown. If they could find it, it would tell the police which way the murderer had gone as he left the house.

There was a small muddy pool opposite the Williams's house on the crossroads.

'I wonder,' said Powell, 'if he threw it in the pool at the crossroads. It would sink in the mud and be very difficult to find.' The sergeant nodded his head, agreeing that it would indeed be hard to find.

The water was not very deep, but the mud was and that made it a formidable and smelly task. With the chief constable's permission, the task was undertaken. The pond had to be drained of water and then the mud, which stank to high heaven, had to be scraped out and put on the adjoining field. It took four days to satisfy themselves that the knife was not there. It was a great disappointment to all concerned, especially to the inspector who felt that he had found the likely place. All that work for nothing but it had to be done if only to prove that it was not there.

There were days when they were very glad that they had the chalet as an office. It was cold and damp and there was a fine drizzle falling from a heavy grey sky.

'I feel like this bloody weather – cold and miserable,' said the inspector.

'Shall I make us a mug of coffee?' asked Les Smith.

'That's a good idea, Les, and we'll go over our findings again. Perhaps we've missed something.'

With the coffee before them, they studied the findings

which the inspector and the sergeant had accumulated.

Powell looked down the list and read out a useless set of problems.

'The murderer came when no one was about. There appears to be no motive, no robbery, no fingerprints, no rape and no murder weapon.'

'There's nothing to hang a clue on.'

'I'm sure,' said Powell, 'that we're missing something, but what?'

'The doctor did say that he thought the stab wound was caused by something bigger than one of the knives from the set. Do you think he could be right, sir?'

Grudgingly Powell replied, 'Well, he could be right. I don't see how he could tell the stab wound was bigger than the knife.

'I've wondered several times if Mrs Neilson had any enemies,' Powell asked himself out loud.

It was clear that some of the womenfolk in the parish did not like her. She'd been a danger to them. She was attractive and always looked smart and she undermined their confidence regarding their husbands. The menfolk all felt she would be fine in bed and this was a threat some of the women feared. Some were not sorry she had gone. But, to be fair, they would have liked her to take her shop some place else. No one wished her dead. If you are both attractive and successful you are bound to make enemies without trying but they would not come with daggers.

'I think we'll have to have another look in the shop, Les. The knife could be hidden on one of the shelves, among the groceries.'

'Do you think so, sir?'

'Well, it's just as likely as all the places we have searched. We've looked at what we thought were the most obvious places. It could be stuck in a garden bed. We've been assuming up to now that the knife was thrown away but it could have been carefully placed where we wouldn't think of looking, on the same principle that if you want to hide, you hide in a crowd.

'Tomorrow we'll strip the shop shelf by shelf and the drawers and cupboards. I'll get the boys to go over the garden very carefully with rakes and hoes to see if it's stuck in the ground. The rakes will find it if it's there.'

They walked out of the house where PC Eric Willis was on duty. He looked as miserable as the weather.

'Willis, go and find Sergeant Waters. Tell him I want a word.'

'Yes, sir.'

It took Willis a little while to find him. The searchers were carefully searching a deep ditch and hedge row.

'You wanted to see me, sir?'

'Up to now,' said Powell, 'we have been looking for a knife which we think has been thrown away. There is the possibility that it has been placed in a hiding place, like stuck in the garden. I want you and the lads to get some rakes and hoes and go over the garden. The rakes will probably find it if it is stuck in the ground. Lay it on for tomorrow morning. I also want three of the men to help me search the shop. We'll clear the shelves, drawers and cupboards. At least we'll know if we don't find it that it's not in the garden or the shop. You never know. There are places one would never think of looking.'

'Yes, sir, it could well be in either place. We'll get to it first thing in the morning.'

As an afterthought the inspector asked, 'Has anyone looked in the rubbish tip? At least we are eliminating places one by one. We could strike it lucky anywhere.'

'There was no knife among the rubbish,' Waters reported.

The following morning the garden was ripped to pieces. They did not find the knife, but they made a good job of undoing all Joe Morgan's work. Now the garden was a real mess, all Joe's work done for nothing. Sergeant Smith and his helpers faired no better. They did not realize how much stuff was there until they started putting things back on the shelves. Annabel had had quite a large stock, all priced ready for sale. There was no more they could do round the house. There were no clues to follow up. Inspector Powell was getting irritable and short-tempered.

'What the hell did he go and kill her for?' he asked Leslie Smith.

'For no bloody reason at all as far I can see,' said the sergeant.

'That's just it. There has to be a reason. If we can find the reason we will be a long way down the road to discovering who did it.'

'If it wasn't sex and it wasn't money, what the hell else is there?'

'Perhaps jealousy was the motive,' Powell said to his sergeant.

'Jealous of what?' asked Sergeant Smith. 'Her business, her looks, or what?'

The inspector thought a minute, rubbing his chin.

'Her business, perhaps. She was certainly doing well at the other shop's expense.'

'But not to the point of killing her,' said the sergeant. 'In my mind, that is out.'

'That leaves her looks. Now the only people this would affect would be wives with straying husbands but I can't imagine any jealous wife stealing out between 11.00 p.m. and 3.00 a.m. getting out without her husband knowing . . . unless of course he was drunk at the time.'

'Be a hell of a risk for her,' said Smith, 'at both ends, with her husband finding she was missing, and risking not being successful at the other end. If she failed, it would be attempted murder and that would be the end of her marriage anyway.'

'It could have been for sex, when you come to think about it,' said the inspector. 'She wasn't raped, but that doesn't mean he didn't try, and having failed, knowing it would be reported to the police . . . he killed her to shut her up. With all those bruises on her legs it points that way.'

'How else could she have got 'um?' the sergeant added to the theory

'Oh, she could have got them in the fight. Women bruise very easily and it looks much worse than it actually is,' observed the inspector.

'This brings it nearer to a crime of passion.'

'And it brings us to the best answer', said the inspector.

'We'll have to make extensive and searching enquiries. The best motive that seems to tally with the facts is a sex murder and we will keep that in the back of our minds.'

'The next thing,' said the sergeant, ' the significance of the pot of tea. This tells me that she knew whoever it was as a friend.'

'That points to someone local, as I see it,' said the inspector, 'but she knew other people outside the place, so it could just as well be an outsider.'

'We'll have to find a way of contacting her son tomorrow. She must have his address somewhere,' Powell concluded.

'Let's hope it will be a better day than today,' said the inspector with a yawn.

Mrs Olive Taylor, the postmistress, might not have looked after herself as her husband would have wished but she had a good business head on her. And now it was the post office and the paper shop and Olive Taylor had got something good out of a terrible murder. She displayed them on her counter. Olive realized that the murder was news in a big way and everyone in Clehonger would want to read all about it.

Most of the national papers carried the story. *The Daily Reader* gave a short factual account, while the other more popular papers had quite an array of headings to catch the eye: 'Postman finds murdered woman.' 'Woman shopkeeper found murdered.' 'Police hunt for murder weapon.'

Some of the women the reporter spoke to admitted that they didn't like her because she was a successful business woman and the men in the place found her very attractive. Another paper stressed that the bruises on her body, especially her legs, indicated that she was raped or that it was an attempted rape and she'd been killed to shut her up.

Bessy Banks and Maggy Bowlan both thought she was a lovely kind-hearted lady who was fond of children and always gave them a few extra sweets for their penny. Mrs Davies, the ploughman's wife, had said, 'Every time my kids went she always gave um extra sweets.'

The papers were having a field day. What was speculation and what was true was difficult to say but it was good copy and left the puzzle of the murder, the who, and the why, for the reader to determine. The police were baffled. The police doctor was quite sure that she hadn't been raped but his statement had to be verified by the post-mortem.

Olive was in her element. Never before had so many people called in the post office. Most of them had not bought a daily paper before. Some had their names mentioned.

Most people in the place bought *The Hereford Times* which was on sale every Friday. This local paper was put to bed on the Thursday night and was in the shops by six o'clock on Friday morning. Every copy delivered to Olive's post office was sold by nine thirty. The paper stated that the police couldn't find the knife which was missing from the set of six and the inspector in charge of the case believed that it could be the murder weapon.

The Daily Reader had said two days ago that the knife had still not been found. They had even drained the pool outside the Williams's house at the crossroads but the knife was not there.

Olive said, 'I'm glad I don't live there. The stench of the mud was terrible.'

People talked over the murder in subdued voices in Miss Thomas's shop, the post office and the pub. There was a feeling that it could be one of themselves so everyone was very careful what they said. But not a word would pass their lips to an outsider of what they thought or suspected.

The inspector and the sergeant met a wall of silence.

9

Among the many things which Inspector Powell had to do was to find out who was next of kin. He asked policeman Willis to do this by asking among the local people standing about on the road opposite Hazel Chalet.

What was and always had been a quiet lane was now filling up with people and the green grass on the sides of the narrow road was being used as a car park. Reporters were moving fast among the local bystanders, collecting little bits of information as they went, like hungry sparrows looking for breadcrumbs.

Although Ted Banks had managed to get away from the policeman, he couldn't escape the reporters who surrounded him. Really he had experienced a terrible shock and wasn't fit to face a barrage of questions. He kept protesting that he had his letter round to do. Nevertheless, Banks told his story, yet again, of how he found her lying on the floor covered with stab wounds in a pool of blood.

'It was a terrible shock, she was a lovely lady.' When he'd finished he was free to go, only to be stopped again by more of the villagers who had only heard a rumour.

The policeman, who was guarding the gate and preventing reporters and cameramen entering the grounds of the chalet, spotted Joe Morgan in the crowd. He called him with his powerful voice and Joe elbowed his way to him through the crush. They had played cat and mouse over the rabbits but they were not enemies.

'The inspector wants to know if Mrs Neilson had a next of kin'.

'Yes,' Joe replied, 'she has a son called Paul. I believe he works in Cardiff. I don't know that for sure but there's bound to be an address or a telephone number somewhere in the house. I've seen a photograph of him. He's a big man like his father was but he looks like his mother.

'Thank you, Joe. I'll pass this on to the inspector. Watch the gate for me till I get back, I won't be a minute.'

A search was made through the drawers for some lead to Paul Neilson's whereabouts.

'I think this is it,' said one of the searchers. It was now late afternoon. The policeman was holding up a letter he'd found which Neilson had written on the company's note-paper: Weber Electronics Ltd., 21 City Road, Cardiff.

It was now 4.30 p.m.

The inspector rang the Cardiff police explaining the position and asking them to find Neilson at Weber Electronics and inform him about his mother's death.

A police sergeant went to the firm and explained to Paul Neilson about his mother's untimely death. The policeman said that he was so sorry to be the bearer of such bad news. Inspector Powell also was so sorry he couldn't find his address earlier.

'Inspector Powell of Hereford CID wanted me to tell you that there's nothing we can do tonight but it would be very helpful if you could come home tomorrow. You might be able to help him with his enquiries,' he said.

Paul Neilson stood there with an ashen face.

'You'd better sit down for a minute, sir' the police officer suggested.

'Thank you, sergeant. I'll be all right in a minute. It's such a shock. I was at home for the weekend. I can't believe it.' Tears filled his eyes. 'She was so full of life and enjoying running the shop.' He turned away and gazed out of the window.

'Please tell the inspector that I'll be home as soon as I can tomorrow.'

By half past ten on the Wednesday morning a weary man

introduced himself to the policeman on duty.

'Good morning, officer. I'm Paul Neilson, son of the deceased. Can you take me to Inspector Powell, please?'

'I think he's in the house, sir, I'll have a look.' As he turned to the house the inspector filled the doorway.

'Are you looking for me?'

'That's 'im,' said the policeman.

'Yes, inspector. I'm Paul Neilson.'

'I'm glad you've come. I'm in charge of this investigation.'

Paul had regained his composure after the shock of last night. He'd left Cardiff at 7.30 a.m. and now it was shortly after 10.15 a.m.

'The first thing I want to do is make a cup of tea,' said Paul.

'That's a very good idea I'll have one with you,' Trevor Powell said.

'We can talk while we drink it,' said Paul as he went into the kitchen to put the kettle on.

There was a framed photograph on the mantelpiece of Annabel and a man, and, having seen Paul, Inspector Powell rightly concluded that the man in the photograph was his father. He would not have recognized her from her battered face. He could see a strong likeness of Annabel in Paul. There was no doubt whose son he was.

'That's Mum and Dad in happier times.'

'I was just thinking that you do look like your mother but you are tall like your father.'

'I suppose there is a lot of both our parents in all of us.'

'What do you do for a living, if you don't mind me asking? You know what I do,' said Powell.

The kettle started to whistle.

'I'll make the tea,' said Paul. Powell followed him into the kitchen.

'No, I don't mind you asking. I'm an electrical engineer. At the moment a team of us are working on a new automatic washing machine. We're what are called the backroom boys. When we've got it right we will send it to Betterclean. They are waiting for us to produce it so that they will be one step ahead of their rivals. We have rivals too. There are several

94

groups trying to perfect a machine which will wash, rinse and dry on a programmed basis. Often, when we have an idea which has to be tested, we work all hours.

'It's exciting and frustrating, at the same time. It's most exciting when it works.'

'It's similar to my work. I search for clues, as you search for successful methods for your machines,' the inspector said.

Paul broke the temporary silence.

'How did the murderer get in? Mother always made sure the door was locked and the windows fastened before going to bed.'

'The front door was open when Banks, the postman, got here at 7.30 a.m. and the key was in the lock on the inside. That's how he got in. The only conclusion we can draw from that is that your mother knew him, and let him in,' Powell replied.

'This brings me to one of the questions I was going to ask you. Have any idea who she would let in so late at night, man or woman, and offer that person a cup of tea?'

'I would think it was a man. Someone would have to be strong by the bruises she sustained. The only person she mentioned over the weekend, was Joe Morgan. She thought he was attractive but, she added, he was married and not for her. He used to give her a rabbit every now and then and he did the garden for her. She paid him for that, of course. Mother was a good Catholic and wouldn't encourage Joe.

'If he'd been single that would be another matter, she told me.

'She mentioned how helpful Father Patrick had been. She was one of his congregation and he called from time to time.'

'What about strangers?' Powell asked.

'I wouldn't know,' said Paul. 'She always got on well with gypsies. Some had been camping near the brook over the weekend. They only came in for shopping. They seemed harmless enough. I don't come over every weekend so I'm not really of much use to you. Mother didn't entertain. She was too busy during the day, and too tired at night for entertaining.'

'I have been thinking, could I use your house as my headquarters while I continue my enquiries?' the inspector asked.

'That's all right by me. I hope you catch him, that's all,' Paul said with anger in his voice.

'Why did you say "him"?' the Inspector asked.

'For no particular reason, it just seems more natural to say "him" than "her".'

'The postman found her yesterday morning. It has been established since, that she was stabbed so it could be a man or a woman. She was not raped. This is private information at present until the inquest. Although she was not raped, the killer could've tried, we think, because of the bruises on her legs.

'I have to see Ted Banks to get his report. He was the first one to find her. Banks rang up PC Willis, whom you spoke to just now. He's the local policeman, who came as soon as he could and by 10.30 a.m. yesterday I came with the Murder Squad,' the Inspector told him.

'I'm afraid they've turned everything over but it had to be done. Up to now we have no clues or fingerprints nor the murder weapon.

'Did your mother ever mention anybody she had had dealings with, or did she mention any bad feelings. Anything to give us a lead?'

'No, nothing like that.'

'What about Henry Roberts?'

'Henry Roberts? Who's he?'

'He's the one who ploughed up the footpath. Your mother took a petition to him and he ordered her off his land.'

'No. She never mentioned it. What happened?'

'The village people took him to court and he was made to put the path back again. He lost his case and had to pay all the costs.'

'No, Mother didn't even mention it, so it didn't mean much to her.'

'What about Miss Thomas?'

'Oh, she might have been a bit put out but she wouldn't do

96

anything like that. In any case, she is too old to tackle Mum. Mum was strong and full of energy. Bad feeling is one thing, murder is something quite different.'

'Your mother never had any trouble with the gypsies?'

'No, not that I ever heard of. One or two came into the shop, while passing through for groceries.'

'Mrs Williams believes all good gypsies are dead ones, they are only good because they are dead!'

'Mother did not share her views about gypsies.'

'I'm afraid you'll have to identify your mother's body. She's in the mortuary in the general hospital.'

The nurse unlocked the door for the two men to enter the mortuary. Neither spoke. Paul thought the bare walls spoke of emptiness and silence. There she lay, covered with a sheet. He went over, lifted the corner of the sheet and looked at her silent, peaceful face. No blood now. She was very pale. He stood and cried. She was silent for ever, now – an unbelievable contrast to what he had known ... a lively sparkling personality. Only a day or so ago she was alive and full of life as usual. He cried again as he let fall the sheet which covered her face. Even the inspector was moved. He came and put his arm round Paul's shoulder and led him away from this sepulchre, back into the world of the living.

Trevor Powell felt very sorry for Paul and made an excuse to leave him alone for a while.

'I'm going to the station. I've some reports to hand in. I'll be back in half an hour.'

'All right, inspector.' Paul was glad to be alone with his thoughts for a little while.

It was a terribly painful experience to see his mother dead. It was a terrible moment he would never forget. It was intensified because he had been home at the weekend and now she was dead, murdered on Monday night. Murder is so sudden and death so final.

It only seemed like yesterday when they were together talking things over about his work and her shop. They could talk to each other and know that what was said would be safe.

She was not considered to be one of the locals ... she was a stranger and that would never change.

However, people had been quite friendly and they did talk about the goings-on in the place. They were always careful because things can get passed on and often spiced up a little. 'I heard...' but they never could remember who it was that said it.

One of the topics which had come up for discussion was holidays. Paul had been making enquiries about the seaside, places like Blackpool or Rhyl, just for a week.

'I wonder,' said Annabel, 'if Vera would come and look after the shop for a week. She knows the ropes. She won't have to do any ordering. I'll ask her next time she comes in.'

'June next year, will that do?' Paul had asked. 'I think that with this much time I can manage to arrange that at work.'

'We have plenty of time to find out about trains and buses and get it all planned well ahead,' Annabel had said.

Then Paul remembered asking about Rob Sadler.

'I hear he's a bit randy.'

'Not with me,' Annabel said. 'I put him off before he started. I was ice cold and he got the message.'

'Good,' said Paul, 'there's no trouble there then.'

'No, everything is all right. I have no one owing anything, and that's something. I'm better off without their trade than with it, if I'm always chasing my money.'

'Oh, you are getting tough, Mum. But I agree with you, things can get very unpleasant where money is concerned.' He had paused, then asked, 'What is Father Patrick like?'

'Very nice, I'd like him more if he was free to marry.'

'Oh, you could like him in that way?'

'Well, yes, he's very charming but wishful thinking gets you nowhere. He's married to the church and that's that. What about you?' Annabel had asked.

'I'm not ready to settle down yet, Mum. It's a tall tree to climb but electronics are the coming thing, especially in television. There's a new thing called a transistor which will revolutionize the industry and soon colour television will come. There are new developments coming all the time.

Everything is moving so fast that it's a full time job keeping pace with the new inventions. To answer your real question, I have my eyes open but up to now I've not been driven by love into a girl's arms. It will happen one day. Miss Right will come along. Actually, I haven't the time at the moment. What with experiments and study, time just vanishes and before I know where I am it's the weekend again.'

'Never mind' Annabel had replied, 'all the work will pay off in the future.'

It had been a very happy weekend. I still can't believe she has gone, he thought. It's a bad dream that won't go away. Yet the terrible thing is I know that it's real.

'I feel a lot better now,' he told the inspector. 'Life has to go on. I've got a lot of things to do but first of all I must see Walter Taylor about the funeral arrangements.'

'It's a good thing to be busy. You haven't got time to brood over the past,' Powell said.

'I suppose you're right, I certainly have a lot landed on my plate at the moment. I daren't think about the property and its contents,' Paul said.

'My Dad used to say, "One thing at a time is quite fast enough." I'll be at the funeral and there'll be some plain clothes lads there as well.'

'Thanks for your kindness at the mortuary, inspector.'

Three days later Paul thought he'd make a brief call on the inspector.

'Can I come in?' Paul said as he put his head round the door.

'Yes, of course,' replied the inspector, 'have a seat.' As Paul sat down he asked, 'How are things going?'

'They're not,' said Powell. 'We really have very little to go on. We've gone through it so many times. Even nature is against us. Not only was the murder committed at night but there was thick fog at the time, so if anybody was about they'd be hidden in the murk.'

'I'll go and put the kettle on and we'll have a break and I'll get a tin of biscuits out.'

'I'm sure a good strong cup of coffee will do us all good,' said the inspector.

As they sat round the kitchen fire, Paul told them the problems his team was having trying to make an automatic washing machine. The team he was working with was under the pressure of competition with other back room boys. The tension and the pressure and the frustration was their common experience. While the officers were thinking about Paul's problems they were having a rest from their own.

'Do you know?' Paul said, 'I've got a funny feeling that there's something missing here.'

'What do you mean?' Les Smith asked him.

'I don't quite know but I'm sure that something normally here in this kitchen is not here now. I can't think for the life of me what it is. I'm quite annoyed with myself. Sorry, it's silly of me'

'Perhaps it's money you've put in a safe place and you can't remember where the safe place is,' said Powell. 'We'll all have a drink in The Plough when we find it.'

'You're on,' said Paul, 'but first let me find where I've hidden it.'

They felt a little better as they returned to their different problems.

Eric Willis was most uncomfortable standing round and waiting for his inspector's command. He was on guard keeping out those who did not want to go in. He felt like a little bit of officialdom no one wanted. He did his best to look as if he were the most important official there. At last he was called.

'Willis,'

'Yes, sir?'

'Go and tell Mrs Banks that I would like to see her husband when he comes home.'

When the message came that the inspector of the CID wanted to see her Ted, Mrs Banks went all hot and excited and was proud that her household was important and her Ted had vital information which the inspector needed.

Mrs Banks said in her most authoritative voice, 'I'll send him round as soon as he gets 'ome.'

The policeman thought, 'She wears the trousers in that house.' What with dogs and geese and the dragon at home poor Ted didn't have much of a life.

When Ted arrived home he found Bessy in a real state of elation.

'The inspector wants to see you as soon as possible.'

'He said he might want to see me again,' he answered. He had never felt so important. The last time was thirty two years ago when he walked down the aisle with Bessy on his arm as his bride. She was slim, tall and an attractive happy bride. He'd always been attracted to tall slim women and at last he'd got one of his own. He'd learnt since those happy days that he would have had many more happy days if he'd been a little bit taller, say seven inches. He could have stood up to her eye to eye. She wouldn't have looked down on him in more senses than one.

Now the inspector wanted to see him again. He was important again and she had to look up to him and he intended to make the most of it.

'I've got your meal all ready for you. Sit down and you can have it right away.'

'All right, dear, there's no need to be in such a hurry.'

'Oh, indeed there is. You mustn't keep the inspector waiting. Your information is very important. You will be helping to solve a terrible murder which happened right under our noses. Now, you just eat your meal and I'll put out your Sunday suit and polish your shoes.'

'Bessy, will you stop fussing. My shoes are polished enough.'

'There's plenty of hot water in the kettle for you to have a wash with that nice smelling soap.'

'I prefer the carbolic.'

'Well, you're not having that. It smells like as if you've come out of hospital.'

'Oh, all right. You're making a lot of fuss about nothing.'

'I'm very proud of you. You are an important witness. You found the body and kept inquisitive people away until the policeman came. Don't you forget to tell the inspector that. Until the policeman came you were in charge and you did your duty very well.'

The inspector was charming. He was on his own so Ted felt there was on one else listening to what was being said.

The inspector said 'I'm very pleased you've found time to come and help me with my enquiries.' He opened a drawer and produced a whisky bottle and two glasses. 'Do you like your whisky straight, Ted?'

'Yes, please, sir,' Ted had never been treated so well before and in return he was only too willing to answer all the questions as best he could. The inspector knew that Ted Banks would be the last one of the local people who would talk. All the others were very careful what they said. Mostly their answer was, 'We don't know that, sir.' As he drained his second glass, the policeman had got all his information plus the repeats. Sergeant Smith, sitting within earshot in the sitting room next door, wrote down most of the interview.

When Ted returned home, Bessy smelt the whisky and Ted was in a happy but sleepy mood. She had learnt over the years to treat him very gently when he was 'in the drink'. Although she was dying to know what happened, she brought him a cup of coffee. But Ted had already fallen asleep. She made up her mind that she'd ask when he woke up.

Mrs Banks was determined to get it all out of Ted that night. She felt he'd told everyone but her.

'Was her face cut?' she asked.

'No.'

'You said there was blood everywhere, in the sitting room too?'

'No, I didn't see everywhere.'

'Do you think anything was stolen?'

'No, I don't think so.'

'What did Eric Willis say when he saw the body?'

'He was 'orrified.'

'Were 'er eyes still open?'

'Yes, dear, but I can't keep mine open. Go to sleep. We've to be up at six o'clock.'

'Oh, very well. I'm the last person to know. To get any information out of you is like trying to get blood out of a stone.'

Apart from the horror of it all, it really was Ted's day. He felt a good six feet tall instead of his five foot three inches.

A postman's job was not everyone's cup of tea, what with the unpredictable dogs, not to mention the vicious ones which went for postmen. He hated ganders as much as the dogs. When he was three years old a gander had knocked him down in a farmyard and stood over him flapping his wings. Ted had been screaming his head off, absolutely terrified, and was still terrified of ganders. He had a strong desire to run when he had to face one. That was why he carried a stick. It gave him a sense of protection. But being a postman was a living. At the moment he was the centre of interest and he loved telling the gruesome story in The Plough Inn as many times as people would want to hear it, accepting a pint or two to help the details along.

The beer and the company helped Ted to forget the dogs and the geese and the dragon at home for a little while. Annabel's murder had pushed him to the front.

Ted Banks was a little man but he'd grown in stature both at home and among his neighbours.

As Ted walked his long letter delivery round he wondered if he'd said too much. The whisky was strong and he wasn't sure what he'd said. The only comfort he found was in the fact that the inspector was also drinking the same whisky and there was no one else listening to their conversation.

10

When Banks had gone the sergeant came from the other room with ample notes of what the postman had said.

'I didn't think he'd tell us much. You didn't see how his expression changed as he answered my question about enemies?' Powell said.

'They don't tell on each other,' said Smith, 'but they have their opinions which they keep to themselves. Mind you, it could be a local person. They don't know if it was one of them. Secretly, they have their suspicions about one or two.'

'They've got to be careful, unless it can be proved, they think it is better to be silent and keep their suspicions to themselves,' the inspector said.

The police knew that the situation was difficult. Powell was an outsider and he was to be kept at arm's length. This was brought home to him and the sergeant when they went for a drink after a hard and frustrating day. The pub looked warm and inviting but the landlord did not smile or greet them.

'Two pints of bitter, please,' said Powell. They were poured out in silence and Powell put down a ten shilling note and waited for his change. Sergeant Smith took the glasses and headed for an empty table.

Powell noticed the landlord's coldness which by this time had spread through the taproom. All talking had ceased and then it started up again in subdued tones.

The atmosphere was uncomfortable for all concerned. Within twenty minutes two thirds of the drinkers had melted away, much to the annoyance of Tom Walker, the landlord.

They noticed that Ted Banks was the centre of interest at a

table where six others were listening to him. Ted had dried up temporarily, then he started again, only now he was talking in a lower pitch. He had three pints in front of him and he had already reached the point of not caring what Bessy Banks thought or said. It was on Friday nights that Bessy did not throw her weight about because Ted could be very nasty when he was the worse for drink.

'I don't like you going to the pub. The drink doesn't do your stomach any good. The doctor did warn you.'

'It's the only pleasure I've got. To hell with the doctor. I wouldn't put it past you to have put him up to it,' he'd say and out he would go before a row started.

When he returned he was ready for one. It was the only time that she was frightened of him and Bessy was careful what she said in case he started throwing things. Many a nice piece of china had ended up in small pieces because she could not keep her tongue quiet. When she got him to bed he went out like a light.

Ted Banks had never been so important. He had never been the centre of interest before. He had so much to drink that Saturday night that his friends had to carry him back to Bessy who led the men to their bedroom where they undressed him and put him, unconscious, to bed. He remembered nothing of it, he was out to the wide. When he woke up to the call of nature at 4 a.m. he was crawling under the bed for the chamberpot and the language would have frightened Satan if he had not taught him the words himself. He fell back onto the bed and the minute his head touched the pillow he was fast asleep again and Bessy had to get up and put the rest of him under the blankets. She had a terrible night.

At ten o'clock he sat up holding his head in his hands.

'Thank God it's Sunday morning. My head's killing me.'

'And so it should.'

'She's off,' he said, out loud.

'And I have a right to be, Ted Banks, with you coming 'ome in such a state.'

' 'Ow did I get 'ere?'

'Four men brought 'yer and put you to bed. I certainly couldn't.'

'Now, Bessy, I know I sometimes drink too much but I've never been brought 'ome like that before. Someone must have put vodka in my drink. I don't remember a thing.'

'If you 'adn't been so full of your own importance it would never 'ave 'appened. You only think about yourself. How dare you treat me in this way? I cook and clean and wash your clothes and run round after you and this is the way you thank me.'

'Don't go on, Bessy, I didn't know they were going to spice my drinks.'

'You're only saying that. You don't know if they put vodka in your beer. You drink far too much and you make me so ashamed.'

'Oh, shut up, for God's sake! My head is killing me.'

'Serves you right. You'll never learn!'

'They kept asking me to tell them more and so I made some of it up as extra.'

'I 'ope you haven't got yourself into trouble by saying things that weren't true. That's what gets innocent people into trouble.'

'No, I didn't mention people . . . only things I saw or said I saw.'

'You'd better get washed and dressed in case someone comes to see if you are all right after last night. Don't you dare to come 'ome like that again.'

She went out and came back again with a cup of water and two Aspirins.

'Get these down you and I'll get your breakfast.'

A policeman stood on guard outside the shop. There was just a chance that the murderer might return to the scene of the crime. At 8 a.m. Powell greeted the policeman on duty.

'Good morning, anything to report?'

'No, sir, it's been a quiet and foggy night.'

'It was foggy in Hereford last night. Good job it's lifting now. Let's hope today is more fruitful,' Powell said with a

106

smile as he entered the building, hoping for some help . . . any help.

All the local people knew and liked Eric Willis. He was their copper. The one they didn't like came from Madley. He would run people in as soon as look at them. What they didn't know was that all the dirty work was done by the policeman from outside. The local cop has to live with his neighbours.

'Mind you,' as Tom Oxley from Madley said, having had a brush with the law. 'They can keep Eric Willis. He's a bastard when he comes 'ere.'

The Clehonger people felt that they could approach Eric and even confide in him. As he was doing his turn on watch several people stood and had a word with him and they all expressed their horror at what had happened. One lady did drop the fact that Rob Sadler had hopes there. She knew him. He had tried it on with her when she worked at the poultry farm. She knew some of the girls had fallen for his charms.

'But I wouldn't believe 'e would do a terrible thing like that.'

Another person mentioned Joe Morgan, the rat-catcher.

'He's been doing work for her and they've been having cups of tea together in the kitchen.'

PC Willis passed the thoughts on to the inspector: a straw in the wind, a crack in the barrier of silence. Rob Sadler had his enemies among some of the women and envy and anger from these women's menfolk. The Inspector thought that it was a line of inquiry which should be followed up. Joe, the rat-catcher, was no saint either. He would have to be investigated.

Joe Morgan lived in Lea End cottage. The lane was a dead end past his cottage and the only way to the last field belonging to farmer Wilson. Joe lived there with Doris, his wife. Joe's father had come to Clehonger with his young wife from Tredegar and lived in the tied cottage belonging to the farm. It was here that Joe was born and because of this he was considered to be a native of Clehonger. 'He's one of us,' his neighbours said but his mother and father were always looked upon as outsiders.

Joe was an ideal person to be a rat-catcher. He was very wise about country matters. Man and boy he had served a long apprenticeship studying the wild life: stoats and weasels, hawks and barn owls, badgers and squirrels and foxes. He knew the inhabitants of the hedgerow and the secret spots where he could find white violets. He got as much fun out of catching rats as his white short-haired terrier Toby did. Toby would wag his stumpy tail furiously and with one ear up he'd dart here and there in a frenzy of excitement.

The farmers did not like Joe's rabbit-thieving ways but they were very glad of his expertise and his help in getting rid of the rats, if only for a while. First impressions meant a lot to Inspector Powell. He was seldom wrong in his rapid assessment. 'Five feet 11 inches of slippery humanity.' That's how he summed up Joe but he realized that the man had a charm which would help to put down your guard and have you believe he was honest and sincere. There was no doubt he certainly had charm.

'I've come to ask for your help, Joe,' Powell said.

'Come in, inspector.'

'Doris, put the kettle on. This is Inspector Powell of Hereford CID.'

'Good afternoon, sir. I'll go and put the kettle on.'

'I believe you knew Mrs Neilson quite well.'

'Yes, inspector, I think you can say that. I get the odd rabbit or bird, pheasant or duck from a grateful farmer for my help with his rats and I offered her a rabbit or bird when I had one to spare. You see, I went there for my cigarettes and we got talking and that's how it came about. She was a very charming lady and it gave me great pleasure to pass something on which I had received.'

'Do you take milk and sugar?'

'Both, please.'

Mrs Morgan poured out the tea and went back to the kitchen.

'Now, I'm not concerned about your poaching. The last

108

time you were caught is still fresh in our minds. But it does mean that you can help us because you are about when other people are tucked away in bed.'

'I've got two more dogs. I'd feel lost without them. I like taking them for a walk before I go to bed, inspector, and sometimes it's late when I take them out.

'I've finished poaching, I can't afford it, especially with the threat of prison next time. My Doris played hell about the fine. She'd divorce me if I went to prison.

'I still take the dogs out, however. It's a good healthy habit of mine now. They might start up a rabbit but even if they catch one they're not retrievers.'

'Let me get to the point, Joe,' said the inspector. 'Were you out on Sunday night ... Monday morning of this week?'

'Yes, I was. It was foggy. It always is this time of the year. It would be between half past twelve and half past one. There wasn't a soul about. It was very quiet.'

'That means, then,' said Powell, 'that it could have happened between half past eleven and half past twelve or between half past one and three o'clock.'

'I walked the dogs round past her place and all seemed quiet. You see, inspector, when it was discovered that she had been murdered I thought back carefully so that I would remember if I were asked. I was quite fond of her, so I just kept my eyes open, her alone with the shop and all. I 'ad no 'idden ambition, just neighbourly like, that's all.'

'I believe you. You did some gardening for her?'

'Yes, I was just getting it straight.'

'Sorry I have had to undo all your work. One last question. Did she have any callers after six o'clock of an evening?'

'Well, she had me now and then when I took her a rabbit or a bird, and she would give me a cup of tea.

'Father Pat, the Roman Catholic priest called after six o'clock when I was having a cup of tea one evening. When he came I finished my cup and went. I'll keep my eyes and ears open, inspector. Gypsies have been in the area and they moved off on Monday. They went Kingston way.'

'Thank you, Joe. You've been a great help.'

'Thank you, inspector. I hope you catch whoever did it. She was a lovely lady.'

From Birch Hill farm there was a wonderful view, which even Inspector Powell could not ignore, despite the pressure he was under. The Black Mountain ridge stood out clearly on the horizon like a formidable barrier protecting the Welsh from the English. Beautiful Herefordshire's wooded hills, like Credenhill, were visible in the middle distance to the right. They stood out purple-blue in the shadow of a big cloud and as he turned still further to the right, Dinedor stood out like a sentinel guarding the city of Hereford.

'On a clear day,' a local told him, 'from here you can see Dinmore hill which blocks the view of Leominster to the north.'

Living in such a beautiful spot, it was hard to realize that a brutal murder had taken place.

Rob Sadler had quite a big flourishing business. Each field had several fowl houses. The different breeds were kept in separate fields. Some of the birds were for meat and others were for eggs: Rhode Island Reds, Buff Orpingtons, Jersey Whites and Wyandottes.

'Funny how people like brown eggs better than white. There is no difference in quality,' Rob tried to explain.

One man told him why he thought brown eggs were better.

'Because,' he said, 'people think of them like bread. We are always being told that brown bread is better for you. I think that's where the idea comes from.'

A lady answered the door bell.

'Yes?' she said. 'What can I do for you?'

'We would like to see Mr Sadler if he's about.'

'Oh, I'm Mrs Sadler. He's in one of the sheds over there. He's culling out the broilers. I'll go and find him for you.'

'That'll be all right, we'll find him. Sorry to have troubled you. Oh, by the way, I'm Inspector Powell and this is Sergeant Smith. We're making enquiries about Mrs Neilson's death. We hope that Mr Sadler may be able to help us with our enquiries.' Mrs Sadler went quite pale. Her anxious look was not missed by the policeman.

'I'm sure that he will help if he can,' she said with a half smile. They thanked her again and headed for the shed she had indicated. They could hardly go wrong for the noise the hens were making was a sure indication which shed he was in.

11

Inspector Powell opened the shed door and as he did so a terrified hen darted out. The inspector was taken by surprise and he wasn't quick enough to stop it.

'Blast!' he said out loud as he squeezed through the partly opened door and quickly shut the door from the inside.

He could hardly see Sadler and his helpers for dust, feathers and flying hens. As he had learned in the forces long ago, there is no retreat so he advanced into the mêlée and noise. The dust was coming up from the litter which was being disturbed by the wings of the frightened birds and the men trying to catch them.

Powell got hold of one of the three men and shouted, 'Mr Sadler?'

The man didn't speak but pointed to another man. Powell nodded and went over.

'Mr Sadler?'

'Yes,' he shouted.

'Can I have a word with you?' holding up his ID card.

'Right, just a minute.' He walked over to one of the other men and said something to him and when he'd put the three hens he was holding into the wire cage he returned to the policeman and pointed to the door. He beckoned Powell to follow him out of the dust-filled henhouse.

When they reached the outside Rob Sadler said, 'That's better,' as he tried to brush the dust and fluffy feathers off his clothing.

'I am sorry to bother you when you are so busy. Your wife told us you were here.'

'Now, inspector, it is inspector isn't it? How can I help you?'

'I believe you knew Mrs Neilson fairly well. You sold her eggs.'

'Yes, that is correct. How did you know that?'

'I saw the empty crates with your name and address on 'um,' said Inspector Powell.

'Oh, I thought someone had been talking.'

'Talking, Mr Sadler.'

'Well, trying to pin the murder on me.'

'Now why should anyone want to do that.'

'I don't know the answer to that one. I'm only guessing. We've all got people who don't like us!'

'What was your relationship with Mrs Neilson?', Powell asked.

'Purely business, Inspector. Mind you, she was a very attractive woman, physically and mentally. I, like many of the lads, would not have minded having a night with her. No, my relationship was purely business.'

'How often did you see her?'

'Twice a week, generally Mondays and Thursdays, with crates of eggs.'

'Would that be in the daytime?'

'Mostly, it would depend how busy we are here. Occasionally I took her eggs in the evening but not very often.'

'Would last Sunday be one of those rare evenings when you delivered the Monday eggs the night before.'

'No, Inspector, not this Sunday last.'

'Where were you last Sunday evening?'

The inspector had unwittingly entered a sensitive and very private area. Sadler had a look round to see if anyone was in earshot before answering.

'I went to the pub about half past eight and went on to see a lady friend of mine for an hour.'

'Has your lady friend got a name?'

'Yes, she has, but I don't want her involved. She is a very sweet private person.'

'Do you think no one knows you visit her when they know how many eggs you have for your breakfast,' he said with a laugh. 'I shall have to know to verify your statement.'

'There is one thing, inspector. If people *do* know, they are being very kind in keeping their mouths shut.'

'I shall still have to know.'

'Yes, I suppose you will, inspector.'

'Her name is Daisy Evans. Don't say anything to my wife about this, I don't want a divorce.'

'What time did you go home?'

'About quarter past ten. Very soon after closing time. I said I would not be late.'

'It is said that you have an eye for the ladies. Would you say that is fair comment?'

'There's plenty more who will have it when they can get it. Between you and me, Daisy is quite sweet and understanding but you promise not to let on. I don't want trouble at home.'

'I'll be as discrete as possible. If Daisy Evans confirms your statement I think it need not go any further. I don't suppose you saw anyone about when you went or when you came away from Daisy Evans's place?'

'No, I didn't. Mind you, it was quite foggy so I couldn't see much anyway. Joe Morgan is out walking his dogs at all hours. He's got good eyes and ears. He needs those for his spare time hobby.'

'And what might that be, Mr Sadler?'

'He catches a rabbit or two. It helps to cut down the farmer's worries of being overrun with them.'

'There's Roger Tomkins, he walks his dog late. He might have seen something.'

'Where can we find him?'

'He works for farmer Morris, up at Hilltop farm.'

'Thank you, we'll have a word with him.'

'It's the fox that worries me. There is one about in the neighbourhood. He got some of Tom Jones's birds the other night.'

'It's being put about,' said Rob returning to the main

subject, 'that Mrs Neilson was raped and stabbed. Is that true, inspector?'

'I'm sorry, Mr Sadler, I am not in a position to confirm or deny the rape theory. It will all come out at the inquest, I've no doubt.'

'It's a terrible thing,' said Rob. 'I really hope you catch him.'

'Why do you say him?'

'Well, if she was raped it could not have been a woman.'

'Yes, yes, I take your point. But the rape has not been established yet.'

The sergeant put away his notebook and the inspector thanked Mr Sadler for being so frank and helpful and wished him good day. He called at the house to ask Mrs Elsie Sadler one very important question.

'Please, Mrs Sadler, do you remember what time your husband came in last Sunday night?'

'It must have been before ten thirty because he had to go to market Monday morning and he has to start quite early.'

'Thank you, Mrs Sadler, that is all.' He gave her a smile and wished her a good day.

As the inspector left the farm, the image of Elsie Sadler's pale and worried face stuck in his mind and he wondered how much she knew of her husband's secret activities.

Daisy lived down Primrose Lane. It had been called that years ago because so many primroses grew on the sunny banks of the lane. She was a cook at the Castle Gate Hotel in Hereford and went there and back daily by bus. Her cottage was surrounded by a variety of flowers in the summertime and looked a picture. She lived in the first of the four cottages in the lane so a visitor did not have to pass the other houses to visit her. It was possible, especially on a dark night, to call there without being seen by anyone.

Daisy had auburn hair and beautiful green eyes. She was a warm-natured woman in her late thirties. Her husband had lost his life in the St Nazaire commando raid on the night of March 27 1942. Daisy had received his VC from the king, but no medal could ever take the place of her Harold. She used to look at it often but now it was put away as one of her sad memories.

She was very fond of Rob Sadler ... an hour with him revived her spirit for living. He was strong and youthful, despite his forty odd years, and it renewed her hopes that she was still attractive. She didn't like cheating on his wife whom she considered was not going short. He had love and to spare.

Inspector Powell also thought that she was attractive as he spoke to her in the soft light of the oil lamp on the living room table and helped by the light of the flames from the coal fire dancing on the walls and ceiling which softened and enhanced her lovely looks. The magic of the moment appeared to be lost on the inspector. His face gave no sign of approval but the sergeant beamed with pleasure. For him she really was something.

'I'm sorry to call on you after you've been at work all day,' he said in a soft disarming voice.

'Can I make you both a cup of tea? It will not take a moment.'

'Thank you very much, but no thank you,' said the inspector.

'I just want to ask you one question and it is in strict confidence.

'Did Rob Sadler come to see you last Sunday evening?'

'Yes,' she said.

'What time did he come?'

'It must have been about nine o'clock and he left about ten. He had to go to market Monday morning.'

'Thank you, Mrs Evans, that's all I want to know.'

'That's the night Mrs Neilson was murdered, wasn't it?' she asked.

'That's right, Mrs Evans, we're just clearing up one or two points. Your confidence will be strictly guarded. What you have told us will go no further.' They got up to go. 'Thank you again,' said the inspector, as they reached the door. 'Good night.'

As soon as she shut the door the sergeant said 'I can't

understand why she's not married again.'

'It's always the way,' said Powell. 'I asked a very attractive lady why she was not married. She answered, "The only men who seem to be interested in me are the married ones or the mother's boys who are looking for a substitute for their mother when she dies." This seems to be Mrs Evans's problem. On the other hand, there are always men about who are sexual athletes who can satisfy three or four women and Rob Sadler is the athletic type.'

Inspector Powell said rather despondently, 'We don't seem to be getting very far. These culs-de-sac are very frustrating.'

PC Willis thought he had better inform the inspector about Mike Lewis who had been out of prison nearly eight months after serving a ten year prison sentence for grievous bodily harm and robbery. It was a very serious unprovoked and brutal attack. He had been drinking earlier in the day and had become aggressive, due really to frustration. He could have killed the man then he would have got life. He had been reasonably quiet since his release, though there had been reports of domestic rows in the house.

The situation was an unhappy one because no one would employ him. If Willis had to go to the house he took PC Ivor Andrews, the policeman from Madley, with him in case he became violent.

'The reason why I have not mentioned it before,' said Eric Willis, 'is because Annabel Neilson wouldn't have taken him through to the kitchen for a cup of tea.'

The inspector said to Willis and Smith, 'Do you suppose he forced her to make a cup of tea?'

'No,' said Eric Willis, quite forcibly. 'He was a beer drinker he wouldn't thank you for tea.'

'That rules him out,' said Sergeant Smith.

'Not quite,' said Powell.

'Why not?' asked Eric Willis.

'She could have had an earlier visitor who had tea and the things were left on the table.'

'How do you account for no fingerprints?'

117

'I don't know,' said Powell, 'unless she or he wore gloves.'

'Why would anyone wear gloves in the house?' asked the sergeant.

'There's no answer to that one,' Leslie Smith said.

'Anyway,' said Powell, 'we'll get him in and ask him some questions.'

The following Saturday morning, the three policemen went to the house at 7.30 and got him out of bed. At first he was a bit aggressive.

'Either you answer questions here,' said the sergeant, 'or we'll take you to Hereford police station and you can answer them there.'

'What's it all about?'

'You answer our questions and you'll find out. Where were you Monday night?'

'Here. Why?'

'Where were you between the hours of 11.00 on Sunday night and 3.00 Monday morning?'

'In bed. You don't think I did Mrs Neilson in do you? That's when she were killed. It said so in *The 'ereford Times.'*

'What proof have you got that you were here?'

'I tell you I was in bed by eleven o'clock on Sunday night.'

'What makes you so sure?'

'That's the time we go to bed. I know nothing about no murder. I've 'ad enough of prisons. All I want is a job and to be left alone.'

'All right, Mr Lewis, we might want to see you again.'

But it wasn't to be because that same night he met with a fatal accident outside The Seven Stars. Mike Lewis, being the worse for drink, walked straight into the path of a Midland red bus and the front wheel went over him. It took eight men with all their strength to lift the bus high enough to drag him out. There was only one car outside the pub and the owner and one of Mike's mates took him to the general hospital but he was found to be dead on arrival.

As the driver of the bus told the coroner at the inquest, 'He stepped straight into the path of the bus and there was nothing I could do' and several witnesses upheld his statement. The Coroner recorded a verdict of accidental death and added a warning about excessive drinking.

Powell said to his sergeant, 'I did not think Lewis was the murderer. I think that his stretch gave him time to think and I expect he thought he was lucky he wasn't a lifer. I think he was trying to keep out of trouble. In a way I felt sorry for him. Nobody wanted him because of his record. I'm sorry for his wife and kids.'

'Perhaps they are better off,' said Leslie Smith.

'Maybe you're right there,' Powell agreed.

'I wonder if Tomkins can help us?'

The following day they went to Morris's farm to have a word with Roger Tomkins. Mr Morris answered the knock on the door.

'Good morning,' he said with a smile. He was short and tubby with a weather-beaten face, as you would expect for a man who was out in all weathers.

'I am Inspector Powell and this is Sergeant Smith. We are from Hereford CID.'

'I have heard that you were in the district looking into the Mrs Neilson murder. Will you come in?'

'Well, we do not want to take up any of your time, Mr Morris, but we would like to have a word with Roger Tomkins.'

'We are just having a cup of tea. Are you sure that you wouldn't like one?'

'No, thanks all the same.'

Mr Morris shouted, 'Bob.'

A young man came from the kitchen with his mug of tea in his hand.

'Yes, Dad.'

'Will you take these gentlemen up to the top field where Roger is working. This is Inspector Powell and Sergeant Smith.'

'How do you do?' Bob said. 'Yes, come with me. Not a bad day for walking through the fields,' Bob Morris remarked as they set off. Not much passed between them as they threaded their way between cart ruts and thorns.

Roger was laying a hedge. Anyone with a trained eye could see that he was an expert at his job.

'This is Inspector Powell and Sergeant Smith from Hereford police,' said Bob.

'Good morning, sir,' said Roger.

'We would like to ask you a few questions.'

'Oh yes,' said Roger.

'Can you remember where you were last Sunday evening from about eleven o'clock onwards?'

'It's about the murder is it? I would like to help. She was a nice lady. I went to the pub about a quarter to ten and stayed with my second pint till ten thirty when I went home and took my old dog for a walk. He's twelve years old and he loves a walk before he goes to bed. I must have got back about twelvish. It was foggy, I remember, and all seemed very still and silent. Although I could not see much in the fog, I have good hearing and my dog has better hearing than me. If he had heard anything his ears would have shot up. I'd swear nobody was about. Most people go to bed between ten thirty and eleven thirty round here. Last Sunday evening Mrs Neilson's light was still on at eleven when I walked round that way. I know the priest from Menbolt Abbey used to call fairly frequently and sometimes Rob Sadler would call with some eggs. She also had the occasional caller for something out of the shop after closing time. She was very good like that. She wouldn't see anyone stuck for something. No one round here could have done this. Was she raped?' he asked.

'We do not know the answer to that one but it will come out at the inquest, I've no doubt,' said the inspector. 'If there is anything you can think of, please let me know. Any little detail could give us a vital clue. If you hear of any strangers being about, please let me know, and their description will be a great help.'

They thanked him for his kind help and promise of more.

'You're doing a fine job here with this hedge. You've been at it a long time I've no doubt.'

'Yes, sir, many years. They say practice makes perfect and

120

I'm still trying. The proof comes in the spring when the hedge starts to grow. That's when you see your mistakes. The bits that don't grow.'

'Well,' said the inspector, 'I doubt if there will be much wrong here. It looks like what it is ... the work of a master craftsman.'

The police hadn't got any further with their enquiries but they had made one farm labourer so happy and proud because his work was praised by such an important person as the inspector.

As they parted Roger Tomkins said, 'If I hear anything I'll let you know.'

'Thanks,' said the inspector.

12

When they were out of the field the inspector said, 'I think we had better go and find the gypsies.'

The Irish tinkers, commonly called gypsies, visited Clehonger and set up camp over the period of the murder. They arrived on the Thursday afternoon. They had wandered their way across country at a leisurely pace. The horses dictated the speed of travel. They chose the country lanes where they could stay overnight without being troubled by the authorities. From the Callow hill they bypassed Allensmoor and, crossing over the Hereford–Abergavenny main road, they headed for their first stop in Clehonger. They halted on a piece of spare ground by the roadside in Gosmore Lane.

As they ambled along from one camp site to the next they had been making pegs. The menfolk cut the hazel wood from the hedgerows and the children peeled the bark off and then the men cut the sticks into peg lengths with tenon saws. Then they were shaped into pegs and fastened with thin strips of tin round the top so that they would not split. They all worked together and a large number of new pegs were already for sale.

On the Friday all houses on Gorsty Common were visited by the gypsies and they sold every peg they had made. Also on the Friday the men went out with their drays and visited the farmers whom they had not seen for a year, to buy any scrap. During the previous twelve months there was generally something the farmer had discarded and was glad to get a small return for.

The boys and girls busied themselves making paper or wooden flowers which the women took round to sell and ask for any old clothes. They always looked as if they really needed them. In actual fact, they are a very industrious people and not poor by any standard.

As soon as they enter a village, however isolated their camp may be, the people who live in the area make sure that all their movable things are secure, in case they might disappear.

Things always seem to vanish when the gypsies are about. Sometimes they are blamed for a neighbour's light-fingered-ness.

'Some of the local people think gypsies are crafty thieves but how far from the truth can you get?' Joe Morgan said to Fred at the cycle shop.

'I agree with you, Joe. They do not harm no one. They only take bits of things no one else wants. Tidying up the place you might say,' said Fred in his present company, knowing that Joe was as crafty as any gypsy. Joe knew Fred talked with two tongues. Fred made sure that his shop and sheds were locked and bolted, gypsies or no gypsies. He had no bits of things *he* wanted stealing.

These particular didicois consisted of four families who had intermarried. There was Tom Taylor and his wife Ann; Bert Smith and Molly his wife. Reg Taylor, Tom's son, married Bert Smith's daughter Betty, and Smith's other daughter, Nancy, had married Ron White, another gypsy. They had four caravans, two drays, six horses, two piebald ponies and two mongrel terriers. The young married couples had five children between them. As they were in and out of all the caravans, only the families knew which children belonged to whom.

They did their shopping on Saturday morning at Mrs Neilson's shop. Last year they went to Miss Thomas. She was terrified that they would steal from the counter while she was getting something which was not right at hand and when she returned to the counter she looked very hard to see if anything was missing. She did not want to serve them but the temptation of their money was too great to resist. When the bill was totted up, Taylor pulled out a very large bundle of notes from a hidden pocket to pay a £9 bill but she very politely saw them off the premises before she relaxed to her stool at the counter where she sat like a contented frog on a stone at the edge of a pond.

These four families, like other groups, did a large circular tour round the villages they had come to know, collecting scrap metal and collecting any unattached bits they could find. They went to the places they had been to before. They knew the lanes like the veins on the backs of their hands. By the time they had been round them all, it was time to start going round them all again. There were plenty of pickings and a few people liked them. In fact, in some villages the people and the gypsies got to know each other, especially the ones who had their fortune told. The same people wanted their fortune told again when they called. It was mostly the women who gladly crossed their hands with silver and they believed every word, however much the gypsy worked the oracle.

They left their secret welcoming marks on the gates of some people who were friendly and, if they were hostile, they left the mark warning other gypsies to keep clear.

The Taylors and Smiths only stayed for three nights but they did brisk trade with the pegs and the men collected the scrap metal. They looked poor but that was a great con and more often than not it worked.

PC Willis told one person, 'The gypsy tries to avoid trouble which would bring him into the public eye. That would help to make his life more difficult.'

In some places they only stayed overnight because the area was hostile.

On the Monday morning at 7.00 a.m. before the murder was discovered, they were on their way to Kingston and after a day or so they would be going along the Golden Valley to Peterchurch.

Inspector Powell knew that they were not moving very fast and he wanted to catch up with them and ask them some questions. He hoped that they might know something or that they might have seen something to help him with his enquiries.

When Inspector Powell reached Kingston he asked an old man. 'Do you know where the gypsies are?'

'If they are in the same place as they were last year they will be down Mill Lane.'

'Thank you, but where is Mill Lane?'

'The third turning on the right. You can't miss it.'

He followed the instructions and as he walked round the bend in the road both sides opened up with a wide green verge and before him a clear brook, sparkling in the sunshine, crossed the road. The ford was wide but shallow and there was a footbridge on one side of the road for pedestrians.

'They couldn't have chosen a better site. I wonder how many times they've been here before?' remarked Sergeant Smith.

'Is Mr Taylor or Mr Smith about?' The question was addressed to a young man who was grooming a pony.

'Dad, there's someone to see yer,' he shouted. A stocky dark-haired man came out of a caravan.

'Who wants me?' he asked.

'I do.'

'And who be you?'

'Are you Mr Smith?'

'No, Taylor.'

'Well, Mr Taylor, I need some help. I'm Inspector Powell of Hereford CID and I'm making enquires about Mrs Neilson's death.'

'I know nothing about that. Who is Mrs Neilson?'

'She kept a shop in Clehonger where you have been for the past three days. Your wife bought groceries from her on Saturday.'

'Oh, she is Mrs Neilson. You telling me she's been killed?'

'Murdered, Mr Taylor.'

'When?'

'Sunday night or early Monday morning.'

'This is the first I've 'eard about it. We left at seven o'clock that morning.'

'Do you or any member of the family remember hearing or seeing anything that might help us trace the killer?'

'I'm sorry to 'ear Mrs Neilson's been murdered.' Taylor called his wife. 'Ann.'

Ann came out of the caravan, a buxom woman aged about fifty. Her hair was untidy and she looked as though she had been working over the stove.

'Wat-yer-want, Tom?'

'Mrs Neilson, where you bought your groceries, 'as bin murdered.'

'Never!' said Ann in an unbelieving tone. 'When?'

'Last Sunday night. The inspector here wants to know if we saw anything or 'eard anything.'

'No, not that I know of. It were foggy that night so no one could see much.'

'I must tell Molly,' and off she went to the Smiths' caravan.

'The doctor said that she was killed between eleven o'clock and three in the morning,' the Sergeant said.

'That's a bit late for us. We were up at five thirty because we were on the move by seven o'clock.'

'Just a minute. I'll ask around.'

Nancy's boy, Nick, came over.

'I thought I saw something. It must have been near midnight. I was late coming from 'ereferd. I 'ad a puncture and I 'ad to mend it which made me later than I would've been. It was very foggy in parts. I thought I saw a man on a bicycle heading for town. He'd gone in a flash. I don't think it were imagination. I was following the grass verge on my side of the road and whoever it was must' ave been doing the same on 'is side. I did not take any particular notice but I remember it now someone 'as asked.'

'Was it a man or a woman,' asked the inspector. Even a straw of information was of value.

'I think it was a man but really I can't be sure. But it was someone on a bicycle. I only had a fleeting glance and it was swallowed up in the fog.'

'Where was this?'

'It was at the top of the Bowling Green pitch.'

'Thank you, Nick. This information is a great help.'

'I wished I 'ad looked a bit 'arder,' said Nick as he walked away.

Although this new information was encouraging, it was also very frustrating. Nick could not tell if it was a man or a woman and as he did not have a watch he was uncertain of the time. So, on analysis, there was little extra to go on.

The inspector thought that he would call on Miss Thomas and buy some tobacco for his pipe, have a look at her and see what she thought about the murder. He had to bend his back to enter the shop. The door was not very high. As he entered, he was amazed at the large quantity of goods on the walls, on the shelves and hanging from the ceiling. In the midst of it all was a plump little lady with hair turning white but rosy cheeks and an alert mind.

Her shop was a gold mine but no one dare tell her she needed more exercise. Her body was like a barrel of liquid fat and, with all the sitting in the shop at the counter and satisfying a good appetite, was making her ready to be bowled into the next world when her heart gave out. As it was, her chest was bad. The doctor had warned her in his blunt way, 'Get it off or you'll pop off,' but his words fell on deaf ears.

'Have you got any Wills's pipe tobacco?'

'Yes.' And in less than no time out of all the apparent confusion she produced the familiar figured silver papered package with the name Wills written in large letters on the front.

'Good, that's it, I've grown used to this brand over many years now,' he said with a smile. He received a bland look in return.

'Anything else?' she asked.

'Yes,' said Powell, 'a box of Swan Vestas please.' Again it was on the counter almost before he had finished speaking.

'That will be three and sixpence please.' He paid her and went on to say how sad it was about Mrs Neilson's brutal murder.

'Are you any nearer finding the murderer, inspector?'

How did she know him? He'd never clapped eyes on her before. She must have had a very good description from somebody.

He said, 'No, Miss Thomas, and I am afraid no one is safe as long as the person is at large. So make sure that everything is securely locked up and I advise you not to open the door after hours to anybody. It just shows what can happen when you do a good turn to someone.'

'I've learned, inspector, that we live in a very hard world and if you want to succeed you have to be hard with it.'

When they came out of the shop Powell met Bob Evans. He was still recovering from his broken leg. The plaster was off but walking was still difficult and impossible without the help of a stick.

'Good evening, inspector. It's not been a bad day for the time of year. I don't envy you your job,' he went on. 'Most people are a bit scared of being accused of having something to do with this terrible murder.'

'Well,' said Powell, 'there's no need to be scared, there is only one person who need be scared and that's the one who did it.'

'Most of us think,' said Bob, 'that it was a stranger and yet, according to what I've heard, they had a cup of tea together, which points to someone she knew.'

'That's the puzzle,' said Powell. 'She would not take a stranger into her living room and make tea, especially when she was in her night things.'

'It makes you wonder,' said Bob. 'No, I wouldn't want your job.'

'How's your leg?' asked the inspector, changing the subject.

'Painful, although the plaster is off it still hurts and Dr Foster says that it will be some time before it will be right. He told me to walk on it. If he had it, he wouldn't be so keen on walking, I'll tell you. I suppose he's right but it's bloody painful all the same.'

'He's a rum old boy is the doctor,' said Sergeant Smith, 'by all accounts.'

'But he's a good doctor and we are all very lucky to have him. These new young doctors coming up look at us as if we were machines rather than people. Dr Foster knows us as if we were his children and we all love him and trust him. We feel he's one of us and that's how he acts with us. Ah well, I'd better be getting back. The wife will think I've fallen over or something. The best of luck, inspector.' With that he hobbled off in the direction of his home.

The policemen returned to their office in Hazel Chalet and as they drank their mugs of tea they went over all the work they had done. They had eliminated Rob Sadler – his alibi was rock hard. They had found nothing that they could pin on Joe Morgan or Tomkins. The gypsies knew nothing about it until they were informed by the police.

'You can always tell when there's something to hide,' Trevor Powell remarked to Les Smith regarding the gypsies. Powell was quite convinced by their attitude that they knew nothing about it. They expressed genuine sorrow about her murder. As Taylor said, 'She seemed a very nice lady.'

However much they thought about it, there appeared to be no motive and the two empty teacups remained an unsolved mystery. The inspector, who was so particular about details, kept going round and round the problem in his mind. At any odd moment, while eating or during a lull in a conversation, his mind would return to the murder. Really, he was getting unfit to live with.

The villagers whom he had talked to were sure that it was done by a stranger but when he put it to them about the cups of tea and Mrs Neilson being in her night clothes, facts which pointed to someone she must have known, they had no answer to solve the mystery. There was one point of agreement: namely that she had put up a great fight. This was accepted because of the multiple bruises all over her body.

'I think I'll go and have a chat with George Lewis. Perhaps he could do a bit of undercover work. He was a detective sergeant in the Birmingham force at one time. He's probably got one or two tricks up his sleeve.'

'I didn't know that,' said Sergeant Smith. 'He is a dark horse.'

'I don't think any of the villagers know that either,' said the inspector.

'Everybody knows he comes from Birmingham but that was all.'

Smith thought it was a good idea.

'The locals might talk to him where they would not talk to us.'

George was busy planting out some lettuce plants when Inspector Powell called.

'Am I glad to see you, inspector?' he said between breaths.

'If you expect me to do that for you, you're wrong, Mr Lewis, I never did like gardening. It's too much hard work for me.'

'Joe Morgan can finish planting these for me. Come on in. What can I get you?'

'I'd be quite happy with a cup of coffee,' said Powell. George led the inspector into the sitting room and called out to Marjory. Marjory came from the kitchen. Powell thought that she was a sweet and quiet lady, such a contrast to her husband.

'This is Inspector Powell of Hereford CID. I thought he'd come to help me with my lettuce plants.' They all laughed.

'Will you make some coffee for us, darling?'

'Yes certainly. I hope he's not done anything wrong, inspector?'

'Oh no, nothing serious this time.'

'I am glad, I never know what's going to happen next.'

Marjory went to the kitchen to make the coffee and Powell told George why he had come.

'At the moment, George, we are completely bogged down. The whole thing is a nonsense. There doesn't appear to be a motive or reason why Annabel Neilson was murdered. I've had a word with the boss and he approves of me asking you if you'd do a bit of undercover work for us.

'Despite all the facts about the tea drinking in her bedclothes, the local people keep saying that it was a stranger

130

and not one of them. It makes me think that they might know who did it and are covering up for someone local. No one will say a word. Will you keep your eyes open and your ears close to the ground and anything you think important, let us know?'

'Certainly. This is second nature to me but up to now I've heard nothing. Remember, I am considered a stranger too, so there's not much hope of anyone opening up to me. But I'll certainly try.'

Powell fished out of his inside pocket a small black book rather like a policeman's notebook, saying to George, 'What do you reckon this is, George? You can handle it. We've got one or two dabs off it. What's it look like to you?'

'Well, it's a Roman Catholic prayerbook. They call it a missal which is mostly used by the priest but some of the laity have their own. This one has been used a great deal. By the look of it and by the way some of the pages are more worn than the others, I'd say it was a priest's personal one.'

'How do you mean, George?' Powell asked.

'You notice some of the pages are used more than the others which tells me that it is probably used especially for sick communions. The mass is often shortened for the sick and these worn pages substantiate my reasoning. I'd say that it was a well-used priest's missal which either he had replaced or he'd lost this one. As Father O'Hara is the most likely original owner in the area, I'd swear it originally belonged to him.'

'George, this really is the first breakthrough we've had. I want to accept what you've said but before I dare do that I want to know how you know so much about the Roman prayerbook.'

'Missal,' George corrected him.

'All right then, missal,' said Trevor.

'When I was a nipper I often went to stay with my aunt in Stoke and she was a Catholic and the priest called every so often and I picked up quite a bit about the Roman Catholics and, of course, I asked a lot of questions. I never knew that what I was learning would come in handy years later.'

'Now, George, I want you to hold on to the ... missal and when he comes back from Ireland I want you to show him the book and ask him what it is. You'll have to play it by ear and with charm. He might say to you, "I'm glad you've found it." He won't be suspicious of you. He'd be much more wary if one of us asked him, even if he's got nothing to hide.

'I suggest that you invite him to your home for a cup of coffee. Marjory can clear the things away and we'll get more fingerprints and compare the original ones with these new ones.

'In the meantime, I'll check up when he went to visit his mother. At last I think we have a breakthrough. By all accounts the priest visited very often. Perhaps he'd got something going there.'

After the coffee he thanked Marjory and George and Powell said to Marjory, 'We'll let him get back to his planting. He can't wait to get started again.'

Inspector Powell was pleased that George Lewis had joined the team of investigators. At lease they now had a new line of enquiry. How important little bits of information can be.

'I think we'd better have a word with the abbot. He might tell us when he's expecting Father O'Hara to come back from Ireland. The father can tell us a bit about Mrs Neilson. She was one of his flock but I don't think he'll know much about the murder,' Les Smith suggested.

'You'll not get much out of the priest about Mrs Neilson. That knowledge is private and confidential,' said the inspector.

132

13

The old abbey tower stood out proudly in the late morning sunshine. The grey walls had mellowed with the years, like many of the inhabitants of the community it housed.

As Inspector Powell and the sergeant walked up the long drive which was lined with beautiful silver trunked beech trees, a gentle but cold breeze whistled softly through the upper reaches of the now bare branches. The cold snap had removed the last yellow and brown leaves which now danced round the trunks of the trees to the tune of the wind.

Sergeant Smith was enjoying the peaceful walk. The world of traffic noise and smoke fumes and the hubbub of daily life, all seemed far away. He felt that he was treading in a world apart. But it didn't stop him thinking that the journey was a waste of time.

'Its a different world here, don't you think, sir?'

The inspector was deep in thought. He wasn't thinking about the scene but about the murder. He didn't think that it was a waste of time coming here. Then he thought of the men who lived in the abbey. At this point his thoughts came to the surface.

'I wonder,' he said, 'what it must be like to be a contemplative?'

'What's that?' asked Leslie Smith.

'It's one who spends his time thinking about God and the scriptures and this wicked world,' the Inspector told him.

'I can understand them thinking about this wicked world, that's what we do.'

'Yes, but they pray that it will improve.'

133

'Do you think they stand a better chance than we do?' the sergeant asked.

'No, but there's always a chance.'

'We put them in prison,' the sergeant went on, 'but most of them don't get better. They learn new tricks and get better at the old tricks and they just wait to get out so that they can start again where they left off.'

'Well, the monks pray for the wicked.'

'And I'd say,' said the Sergeant, 'we prey on them.'

'You're a cynical bastard at times, Leslie. But seriously, I don't think I could kneel down and wait for something to happen,' said Powell. 'I want to *make* it happen. It's not the life for me but it obviously seems to be the life for them. Perhaps you're right about wasting our time coming here, Leslie, but every stone must be turned over. I suppose the father might, just might, tell us something about Mrs Neilson we don't know.'

'I think we are doing the right thing to see the priest,' admitted the sergeant. 'He knows his flock quite well but I doubt if he knows much about Mrs Neilson's private life. That is if she had one. She was always very busy in the shop ...'

The Inspector cut him off, 'He's not going to tell us anything of a private nature.'

'Yes, I know that. I'm only making the point that he must know her better than most.'

'I doubt it,' said Powell. 'With all the confessions he hears do you think he can remember all he is told? In any case, in the confessional he does not see the penitents' faces. He might know them by their voices but even that's doubtful. By the time he's heard thirty or so confessions before mass, he couldn't tell you who confessed what.'

'Oh, I never thought of it that way. I suppose he couldn't remember what people have told him unless it's a murder or something terrible like that,' said the sergeant. 'In any case, you wouldn't be happy if you left O'Hara out. You'd always be wondering if he was the one who held the key to unlock our problem.'

'Yes, I know you're right. My enquiries would not be complete without the interview.'

When they arrived at the large imposing oak doors with huge iron studs all over them, the sergeant noticed that it looked like the doors he was used to at the entrance to the prisons.

'Ring the bell, Les.'

The sergeant pulled the big shiny brass bell knob. He pulled it twice but no sound reached his ears. He assumed that it must be working. The massive dark studded door gave the impression that it was a symbol of protection for those inside against the world, the flesh and the devil. It was the door of the fortress of righteousness which would prevent the intimidation of the poor in spirit.

The sergeant didn't like to pull the bell knob again in case it had rung the first time. As he waited he looked at the massive stonework and thought of the skill of the builders in those days.

'This must be a very old place,' he said to his boss.

'Older in some parts than others. Elizabethan with additions, I'd say,' said Powell.

'I'll bet it costs a packet to keep a place like this going,' said Les Smith. 'I believe that they are dependent on the large number of congregations which are scattered over a wide area. It's their money which helps to keep the place going.'

As they waited, the inspector felt uncomfortable.

He said aloud, 'The priest wouldn't know any details about her death or why it happened. He'd be tucked up in his little bed miles from the scene of the crime. The interview with Father O'Hara is necessary to complete our enquiry. She was a member of his church. He did know her and from time to time visited her and even if he tells me nothing I don't know, I shall have seen him and interviewed him and it will be recorded as the last of her occasional visitors.'

The wicket door meekly complained about its lack of oil as it opened slowly, revealing the thickness of the great oak timbers. This ancient solid door made the tall thin

135

black-robed monk look quite lath-like by comparison.

'Good morning. I am Inspector Powell of Hereford CID and this is Sergeant Smith. Could we speak with the Abbot, please?'

'Please come in,' the priest said and he ushered them into a large comfortable room full of books.

'Please wait here a moment,' and with that he went out and shut the door silently behind him.

All the walls were bookshelves full of books. There must have been four thousand books there.

'Some reading here,' said Leslie Smith. 'It would take me a lifetime to read all this lot even if I had nothing else to do.'

They stood and looked at the vast collection of books which seemed to cover a great range of subjects. They were just beginning to wonder what was happening when a portion of the bookshelves opened and in walked a stately gentleman in a cassock with a large crucifix hanging on a purple cord round his neck. It would have been like a miracle: first he wasn't there and then he was but it so happened that they spotted the movement and they were not taken unawares.

'Good morning, gentlemen. I am the abbot. Can I help you?'

The inspector introduced himself and the sergeant and told the abbot, 'We wish to complete our inquiries by asking Father O'Hara, who knew Mrs Neilson, to tell us anything he might know about the deceased. She was one of his flock, so I have been told. We know that he is in Ireland at present, visiting his sick mother. Can you tell us, sir, when he is likely to come back so that we can ask him a few questions.'

'I can't give you an exact date, inspector. His mother is making a steady recovery and we hope to have him back within the next few days. Of course, he set off for Ireland before the terrible murder took place. As he was away from the parish at the time I don't see how he can add anything useful to your enquiry. Most other knowledge he has about Mrs Neilson is private and under the seal of confessional. I'll tell him when he returns that you have called to see him.'

With that the abbot stood up, signifying that the interview had terminated.

'Thank you, sir, for giving us your time. We did not think that he could be much help to us but we felt that we must ask. We can eliminate him from our inquiries.'

As the inspector was speaking, the abbot had already moved towards the door to show them out.

'I hope you find the murderer. It is a terrible tragedy.'

As they left the grounds of the Abbey, Smith said, 'He couldn't get rid of us soon enough. He didn't welcome the police on his doorstep.'

'People could wonder what was going on in the abbey,' said the inspector.

'As we are so near Hereford,' said Powell, 'I'd like to call at the railway station and check up when O'Hara left for Liverpool. Just routine but it finishes off this enquiry.'

Powell tapped on the sliding door at the ticket window and a ticket collector slid it open with a bang.

'Yes, sir.'

'Could you tell me please if a ticket was sold on Saturday or Sunday last for Liverpool?'

The ticket clerk looked at Powell a little suspiciously.

'Who wants to know?'

'Inspector Powell, Hereford CID,' and he produced his official card.

The clerk changed his attitude.

'Yes, certainly, sir.'

He left the window and after what seemed a very long time, the clerk returned smiling.

'Yes, sir. One ticket was sold on Sunday afternoon for Liverpool.'

'Was he a priest, do you remember?'

'He was muffled up. Mind, I wasn't taking much notice but I seem to remember that he had an Irish accent.'

'Thank you, you have been most helpful.'

'Well, that's closed another avenue,' said the inspector.

'I still think it's one of the locals. I think the locals think it's one of them but no one is saying anything.'

'Now when they see us coming they quietly vanish in case we ask them questions,' remarked Smith. 'There are no finger-prints, there's no murder weapon, there's no motive.'

'There's nothing,' said Powell.

'What about rape?' the sergeant asked.

'The doctor did not think so and he should know without an autopsy. These fellows know the signs and he said no to rape,' the inspector replied.

'So,' the sergeant said, 'we are left with nothing. We have a lot of statements but they all add up to nothing.'

'A small group of specialists,' Powell said, (really he was thinking out loud), 'Have been sent from Scotland Yard to help in the search for the killer but apart from a few notes and blood samples and helping in the door-to-door enquiries, they've not made any new ground. So they've returned to London and left us to it. It was a waste of money them coming in the first place. They couldn't get away quick enough.'

'That about sums up the specialists,' said the sergeant.

'There is a bus stop not one hundred yards from her shop. I think that I will get a small team of men to question the passengers who used the buses in case they were on the bus on the Monday of the murder. They might have seen a stranger get off at the bus stop,' Powell said.

These inquiries were just as fruitless as the others. The locals kept quiet, perhaps because they did know something, the others outside the parish were tacit because they didn't know anything.

No one seemed to remember anything out of the ordinary.

'Well, we did try,' said Les Smith.

Powell sent two officers to the general hospital to enquire, principally at the outpatients' department, if anyone had come in for treatment for cuts and bruises but there had been no patients needing such treatment.

All the city doctors were contacted. Here too they drew a blank.

'We'll have a rest until Monday,' Powell said. 'I expect there will be a big turnout for the inquest. The kids will be sent home early. They'll have to be if the inquest is going to be held in the school at three o'clock.'

As far as anyone could remember there had never been an inquest for a murder in the parish before, certainly there did not appear to be a record of one. Curiosity did far more to bring the people to it than sympathy. The obtrusive question was not so much who did the murder but how was she murdered and was she raped? They were very interested in the last question. It certainly had been put about that she had been.

'I think,' said Powell, 'that they can visualize rape better than stabbing, or perhaps it's more interesting to them. She was a very attractive woman according to the photograph in the sitting room.'

The main large schoolroom was filled with people all talking at the top of their voices. The table and chair were in place and awaited the coroner. There was an air of excitement. The attraction was multiple. Some people liked to live through the horror as the postman saw it, or as the doctor clinically explained it. Some of the men imagined her fighting in her blood drenched nightie. Was it a stranger to the area, but someone she knew from where she came from?

Annabel Neilson had been a very attractive person and it seemed more than likely that some man was mad to have her, with or without her consent. Did she have a lover? What reason could there be to murder her? The police were still searching for a motive. The air was electric. Would 3.00 p.m. never come?

Powell leaned over and spoke in Smith's ear, 'One would hardly think it was over a woman's brutal murder.'

Quite a number of people couldn't get in. The entrance was blocked. The schoolroom windows were wide open and people were gathered round each window so that they could hear what was being said although they couldn't see the proceedings.

As the hour approached, the signal that things were about to start was the voice of PC Willis making a gangway for the coroner to make his entrance. As he entered the school room behind the policeman, silence fell on the assembly.

Willis in full voice said, 'All stand,' and in the silence he led the way to the platform. As the coroner sat down, once more he shouted, 'Be seated, ladies and gentlemen.'

The coroner explained to all present that this was not a court of law but a court to establish the victim's cause of death.

'First I call Officer Eric Willis to give us his statement.'

Eric Willis really did feel that he was the voice of the law at this moment.

The policeman related, 'I had a phone call from Mr Banks here,' pointing to where he was sitting, and Ted Banks gave a confirming nod, 'telling me how Mrs Neilson was dead.' Referring to his notes, he went on, 'It was 7.45 a.m. when the telephone rang and I told him to wait there until I arrived, which I did in about twenty-five minutes. Mr Banks gave me the following statement. ' "I got to the house with the post at 7.30 a.m. and as the door of the shop was ajar I shouted, 'post', but there was no reply. I pushed the door open a bit and shouted again, putting my head round the door thinking Mrs Neilson was in the kitchen. Again, there was no reply. As my eyes got used to the poor light I saw Mrs Neilson lying at the end of the counter. I thought she had had an accident and went in to see if I could help her and found that she was in a pool of blood. When I got myself together I rang PC Willis and waited until he came, as he told me." '

When the policeman had finished his statement he looked up to where Mr Banks was sitting and Banks gave a nod to confirm what he had said in his statement.

Then he went on, 'I rang the chief constable's office and reported the murder.'

'Thank you,' said the coroner.

Inspector Powell was called to give his findings which made it quite clear she had been murdered.

He said, 'I am very grateful for all the expert help Scotland Yard has given and the army for using their mine detectors and for searching twenty-five square miles to help us find the murder weapon.

'The police have interviewed altogether three thousand people. We are still appealing, sir,' addressing the coroner, 'for help to find the murderer.'

The coroner was more at home with the next witness, the pathologist because he himself was a doctor.

The pathologist said, 'Mrs Neilson met her death by three types of violence. She was partially strangled and beaten about the head but died of stab wounds which caused her to bleed to death. It was not a sex killing, as some thought to be the motive. She had not been raped as it was supposed by the bruises on her legs, which must have been caused in the struggle which, obviously, had taken place.'

There was a quite a murmur and a shifting of feet by the people in the school room when rape was ruled out and quite audible talking by the people standing outside near the open windows and the main entrance door.

The policeman standing by the table where the coroner was seated said in a loud voice, 'Quiet, please!'

Now there was definitely no motive that one could find for the murder.

The coroner, who had seen the body, confirmed what the police pathologist had said and the proceedings were brought to a close with his summing up.

'Mrs Neilson has been murdered by a person or persons unknown.'

PC Willis noticed that people were beginning to move out of the building so he shouted, 'Will you all stand, please.' The movement ceased and the policeman led the coroner out of the school room to his car.

Although people were anxious to get out of the school-room, they were in no hurry to disperse. They gathered in groups and talked over the proceedings. The tension and the excitement had evaporated. Some of those present felt cheated because all the blood and stabbing part of it was played down, really for the sake of the women present, although secretly they enjoyed the gory bits as much as the men. They went away with one thing burning into their memories. She was murdered by a person or persons unknown and so the whole thing was still wide open. The murderer was out there somewhere.'

'There's a good attendance,' said Powell, looking around him at all the mourners who had come to the funeral.

'I'm glad it's not raining for them. I reckon all the people of Clehonger are here.'

'She must have been popular,' said Smith.

'I think there is genuine grief over what happened. There are some beautiful flowers, so some thought a lot about her.'

There was a surprising number of strangers among the mourners who came to the funeral. On closer inspection it turned out that most of them were newspaper reporters and plainclothes police, male and female.

When the service was over and the committal finished, the police stood at both entrances to the churchyard and asked the people leaving for their names and addresses. Perhaps there was someone there who could help them with their enquiries. Here too they drew a blank.

The police made several appeals for information. Names would be kept in strict confidence with the promise of a reward if any information led to capturing the murderer.

Again, this request was met with silence.

14

The requirements of the inquest were positive in their function. The coroner spelt out the verdict with the words, 'Unlawful killing by person or persons unknown'. This was a negative conclusion regarding the murderer. It would appear to be the end of the matter as far as the villagers were concerned. It certainly removed from them the suspense that it was one of them who had done it. This is what most of them believed and secretly, man and wife in bed, out of hearing of the children, expressed their conviction to each other who it was, but now the coroner had said by person unknown. It was a final summing up of all the hard work the policemen and the army had put in. Yet the so-called findings were inconclusive. The woman had been brutally murdered and the murderer had not been brought to justice.

Powell firmly believed that it was someone in the parish; but he, like the rest, had not got an official name of anyone whom they could accuse guilty of murder.

The atmosphere remained tense but no one spoke their private thoughts. The villagers believed that one of them had done it.

Inspector Powell thought that perhaps now some of the tension would ease off and the atmosphere would become warmer but in fact it lingered on. The local people wanted to talk about it, so they started talking about finding someone outside the parish, perhaps someone from the old RAF camp used by squatter families. They felt freer to talk about it if they were not involved. Some outsider did it and that's how it rested.

After all, the coroner had said 'person or persons unknown'. 'Perhaps he meant someone from outside unknown to us local people,' said Joe Morgan to George Lewis and Rob Sadler as they sipped their pint of beer in The Plough.

'It bristles with problems,' George said. He was doing his best to get some clue but nothing was forthcoming. The question was quite baffling.

'What beats me,' said Rob Sadler, 'was that there did not seem to be a reason. If it was theft the police could be looking for a thief who bungled the robbery and killed Mrs Neilson to stop her reporting him to the police. She obviously knew him, or her, of course, but nothing was stolen. The coroner made a point of letting it be known that it wasn't rape, so sex was not the motive.'

'It might well have been,' said Rob, 'she was a real good-looker. I'm glad she wasn't raped.'

'I don't go for this jealous woman theory,' said George. 'She'd have to be very strong and be very cold-blooded and calm to wipe all the fingermarks away before leaving.'

'That's just a load of nonsense,' said Joe. 'A woman would have to be in a rage to do such a thing and being in such a state is hardly likely to wipe carefully everything she'd touched.'

The three agreed that it had to be a man.

Mrs Moss was all smiles when she opened the door to Ted Banks.

'Good morning, Mrs Moss, I have a letter for you all the way from Ireland.'

'Oh, it'll be from Father O'Hara. He said that he'd write and let me know how his mother was. Thank you, Ted, I see you have a catalogue for me. I'll have a read at that this evening, thanks. It's a bit late for a cup of tea. We'll have one the next time you call,' Mrs Moss promised.

'Thanks, Violet, I haven't got time now anyway.'

He liked calling on Violet Moss. She had no snappy dogs that he'd have to contend with.

144

Violet Moss read through Father Patrick's letter. His mother was improving, but her chest was still not right.

'I hope to be back as soon as the congestion clears up.' She read his letter out loud. 'I'd like to have *The Hereford Times* if you'd post it to me. It's good to know what's going on. My home is with you now.'

'I'm glad you feel like that, Father, you belong to us here.' She spoke out loud as though he was there in the room with her. 'I expect you've read the national papers about Mrs Neilson and the terrible murder. No one knows what to make of it. As soon as you go away, Father, something happens. We're all very sorry. Mrs Neilson was a very sweet lady. I'll send you the paper. No, I don't want paying for it. I'll read it on Friday and send it to you on Saturday.' She read some more of the letter aloud. 'I hope to be coming back very soon, in two weeks' time, maybe. Mother's getting better all the time.'

'I'm glad you're coming back soon, we miss you at church.'

The following day was Friday so she went to Olive Taylor's at 8.15 a.m. to make sure she'd get her copy of *The Hereford Times* before they were all sold. Violet told Olive that she'd had a letter from Father Patrick.

'How is he?'

'Oh! He's all right, it's his mother who's ill.'

'Yes, I know. Is she any better?'

'Yes, he hopes to be back soon,' said Violet.

'He comes back to a very troubled parish,' said Olive.

'But he's still glad he's coming back,' Violet spoke for a lot of his parishioners.

'Oh well, life must go on. Do you want anything else?'

'Not today, dear. I'll come and post his paper to the Father tomorrow when I've read it.

'Bye, bye.'

'Bye, bye.'

Father Patrick O'Hara was delighted to have a letter from Violet Moss and *The Hereford Times* which she said she'd send him every week.

145

'It's amazing,' he said to his mother, 'the things that can happen when I'm away.'

He read every scrap that was written about the murder and he was quite surprised that the whole matter was inconclusive.

'It's astonishing how quickly yesterday's news is tomorrow's history,' he said to his mother.

His mother had already lost interest. She was more concerned how the priest, her son, was getting on. She was quite contented to know that he was all right and was happy with the celibate life.

Father Patrick was very pleased to be back, especially among his flock on Gorsty Common. He heard all the gory details of the murder over and over again. Everyone was anxious to tell him and listen to his comforting words. Facing death is bad enough but to face the horrors of murder was an experience no one had had to face before. The worry was that the murderer was still on the loose. Comfort for the bereaved came in the words, 'Time is a great healer,' and for those who worried about the murder he brought solace with these words, 'He'll be punished in the end.'

'When will that be, Father?' someone asked. That was a difficult question to answer. He looked at his watch.

'Oh dear, I'll have to go, I have so many people to see.'

George had waited for Father O'Hara to return from Ireland and for the right moment to bring up the question of the missal.

Another house had been built below the brow of the Birch Hill, beyond George Lewis's bungalow and one of Father O'Hara's parishioners had recently moved in there. George had hoped that he could meet the priest casually one day. The day came when he could catch him.

He'd waited a long time for the priest to come to visit George's new neighbour. George let him pass and after a quarter of an hour he came out dressed to do some gardening. As Father O'Hara was coming back he spotted George in

146

the garden so he stopped to have a word. George spoke first.

'How is your mother, Father?'

'A lot better, thank you, Mr Lewis.'

'Everyone calls me George so perhaps you'd do the same, Father? I've done enough gardening. Come on in and we'll have a drink.'

'Thank you, George, I'd be liking that.'

George led the way into the sitting room. Father Patrick remarked on the wonderful view as he walked to the great window.

'I could stand here all day admiring such a view.' George noticed that his Irish accent was more pronounced than usual!

'What would you like to drink, Father? Whisky, sherry, gin, coffee or tea?'

'I'd like a whisky, George, with a little ginger, please.' George poured out two fingers of whisky and told Father O'Hara to help himself to the ginger.

When they were seated George said, 'I expect you've heard all about the terrible murder. She was such a sweet lady too. They haven't found the murderer or the murder weapon.'

'Yes, I heard the terrible news on the wireless on the Monday midday broadcast. It's an awful thing to happen. No one feels safe these days,' said Father Patrick. 'As long as the murderer is not apprehended no one can feel safe especially those living on their own.'

'While you're here, Father, will you settle something for me.'

'I will if I can, George.'

'I won't be a minute.' George went into another room and returned with a small black book which was like a policeman's notebook.

As he handed it to the Priest he said, 'My friend says this is a Roman Catholic breviary and I say it's a missal. Who is right?'

Father O'Hara turned the pages over and said, 'You're right George it's a missal. It's been about a long time and it has been well used.'

George was watching the priest's face for signs of recognition as he held the book. He noticed that he'd gone a little pale and he seemed slightly nervous but his voice was calm and steady.

He was listening to George when he picked up his glass and bumped his elbow against the side of his chair and spilt some whisky on his clothes and the black book.

'I'm so sorry,' he said as he reached for his handkerchief and wiped the book carefully all over, saying, 'no harm's been done I'm glad to say,' and he handed the missal back to George.

'I'll have to be going. Thank you for your hospitality. I'm glad I did not spill the whisky on the carpet.'

'I hope you'll find time to call again when you're passing, Father. You'll always be welcome.'

'Thank you, George I'll remember that.'

George realised that all, or nearly all, his careful planning to get some more fingerprints were foiled by the accident, or was it deliberate? Father Patrick had been very careful to wipe the missal all over back and front and some of the pages. There might be some fingerprints left, but there were some on the ginger bottle and his glass.

One day when Paul was in the kitchen of the chalet he remembered what was missing. He'd told the inspector that he knew that something was missing from the kitchen but he couldn't think what.

When Paul walked into the inspector's office he said, 'I remembered what I said about something missing in the kitchen.'

'Yes,' said Powell as he looked up from his notes, 'what was missing?'

'The ice axe,' said Paul.

'What ice axe?'

'Years ago mother bought it for chopping up wood. It had a spike on the one end and an axe head on the other. That could very well be the murder weapon.'

Paul said that he'd have a look round to see if he could

148

find it. He looked round the chalet and then in the garden, which he thought would be the most likely place. Joe Morgan had collected firewood and stacked it there. As he searched he saw a bright amber light on the trunk of the damson tree reflecting the sunlight. He went over to look at it, and there, the cause of the amber gum, was the long lost knife. It was stuck in the tree and whoever put it there must have forgotten where he'd left it.

He had the knife in his hand when he went back into the office.

'Look what I've found.'

There was silence in the office. No one knew what to say. The amount of time and labour was more than one could calculate. The inspector asked Paul to do a drawing of the ice axe for him. When he saw the drawing he understood the doctor's doubt. The stab wound would certainly be bigger than a knife wound.

The inspector was completely baffled and thought that he'd better explain the situation to his chief. Perhaps he might have some ideas on how to solve the mystery.

'I have had some tricky problems in my time, sir, but I can find no answer to the question, "why!" The villagers have shut up like the county jail which makes me think they believe one of them is a murderer but it has to be proved and that's another story.'

'Leave it with me. I'll have a word with the Yard about it, perhaps they have some ideas. I have to go to the Yard on Thursday so I'll mention it and see what they think. Just write me out a full report by Wednesday afternoon so that I can go through it first.'

Inspector Powell was really worried because he had all the facts. He had pages and pages of interviews but he felt that someone was being protected. He felt that the whole lot on Gorsty Common were in a conspiracy of silence. If they believed that one of them was a murderer, they might believe that they could be in personal danger themselves if they said anything to anybody in case they said it to the murderer. He

149

might do the same to them as was done to Mrs Neilson if they got too near the truth. Perhaps they were protecting someone else because of their families. Perhaps Mrs Neilson had refused to help someone who was short of money and she would not let them have things on tick. No, that doesn't make sense. If they had been after groceries, the person would have taken them but nothing was missing.

He talked to himself.

'I wish I'd never seen the bloody case.' For a man who was so particular about details he really was suffering. 'The killer was clever. There is nothing. It's like a chapel without hat pegs. There is nothing to hang the smallest clue on.'

Powell set to and produced a ten page document for the chief to take with him to the Yard.

Jim Matthews read through Powell's report, which he had headed:

THE NEILSON MURDER. MONDAY 17th MARCH 1952.

The document brought him up to date with the case. These cases had to be left in the department which dealt with them. The chief constable had so many other things to worry about. There was a big investigation going on concerning a robbery in a jeweller's shop in High Town and a fight outside The King's Head in Widemarsh Street. A man was in intensive care in the general hospital. The other one was patched up and was now in custody. Both these crimes happened on the same Sunday night.

As the chief constable, he kept a watchful eye over all the activities but left the work to the experts in each department to get on with the job. Sometimes they needed extra help and this is where Jim and his other contacts came in.

The Neilson murder now needed his full attention. The investigation had come to a stop like a car running out of petrol on a lonely empty road. Powell could find no help with further information and so at last he appealed to Jim Matthews, his boss. It was a very long report and so before he went to bed Jim read it through again.

'Are you coming to bed, Jim? You've to be off early in the morning.'

'Yes, dear, I'll not be long. I must read this through. It's Powell's report on the Neilson murder and there'll be no time in the morning.'

'Well, hurry up. Have you had your whisky?'

'No, not yet.' He always had two fingers before he went to bed. The doctor said that it was good for him.

'I'll get it for you.'

'Thank you, dear.'

She brought it and put it on the table by his hand.

'Now hurry up, there's a dear.'

'All right, now go on off to bed. I'll be there in a minute.'

'I think that I have got all that matters,' he said to himself. He carefully put the report in his black leather briefcase, finished his whisky and quietly went up stairs.

'You need not creep about, I'm not asleep,' said his wife. He soon hopped into bed beside her.

The alarm clock made such a noise that it was loud enough to awaken the whole street. It was half past six and he felt that he had only been in bed a short time but he had had a good seven hours' sleep.

While he was shaving he was going through the report again in his mind. Then all the other things, like the time of the train, platform 2, *The Telegraph*, tobacco for his pipe, the briefcase, he'd take his light rain-coat in case it rained. All these things flashed through his mind as he dressed.

'Good morning, dear. Did you sleep well?'

'Yes, thank you. Now get a move on. You haven't got time to dally about.'

When the train left platform number 2 Jim settled down to read the paper. The journey was uneventful and there seemed to be only a few people travelling. One or two got on at Oxford and a few more got on at Reading. The train reached Paddington on time. He got a bus to the Thames Embankment and headed for New Scotland Yard Central building which housed the forensic science laboratory, the criminal record office, the fingerprint and photography departments and several other branches of the Criminal Investigation Department.

Jim Matthews hoped that they might have some new ideas on how to break this barrier of silence because Powell was convinced that's what it was and Jim agreed with his findings.

The Hereford chief constable was well-known at Scotland Yard. He'd worked there for a while before going into the country. He liked to keep in touch. When he walked in he was greeted by one of his old pals whom he had known and worked with some years back.

'How are you, Boyo?'

It was Dai Thomas, Chief Inspector now, if you please. He was a fingerprint expert. He had learned his early policing in Barry Dock and although he had been in London many years he was still as Welsh as ever. He always was full of fun.

'Has Wye Bridge fallen down as a result of vandalism?

'No, Dai, I've come specially to see you because they're building a new one way bridge over the Severn.'

'One way? What's that for?'

'If you cross it from England you will not be allowed back. They are running short of good Welshmen in Wales.'

'Now seriously,' said Dai, 'you have a worried look.'

'Yes, indeed. I have a hard nut to crack this time.'

'What kind of nut? Theft, rape, murder, trade secrets, corruption in high places? We thought Herefordshire was immune from most of those things.'

'It's murder,' said Matthews. 'Murder with no motive and no clues and nobody is talking. All I am greeted with is silence.'

'Bill Austin is your man. Up the stairs, turn left, third door on the right. I'll give him a bell to let him know you're coming.'

'Thanks, Dai, I'll get up there. Can't be too long. I've got to get back. 'It's been real good to see you.'

'And you, Jim. I'll call in one of these days on my way down home. My mother still lives in Barry Dock.'

Bill Austin was a tall dark-haired man, ex-Coldstream Guards, in his early fifties. He had been posted to the Murder Squad some three years ago.

Matthews knocked on the door and a voice could just be heard saying, 'Come in.'

'I'm Jim Matthews. Dai Thomas told me to come and see you.'

'Yes, he's just rung me and told me you were coming. You have a cup of coffee while I read through your report. I've sent for the coffee.'

Jim handed over Powell's report and Bill started to read. There was a knock on the door. 'Come in,' shouted Bill. The coffee had arrived, delivered by a very smart and attractive young policewoman.

'Help yourself, Jim. I'll have mine when I have finished this'. When he came to the end, he said, 'Now I know why you've come. It's a sticky one. I'll have to think about it. I couldn't give you a useful reply off the cuff. I'll write to you in a day or so. I'll talk it over with the squad and see what they come up with.'

'Fine,' said Jim.

'How are you liking the Hereford post?' asked Austin.

'It's a bit slower than here,' said Matthews.

'I expect in some ways that you're glad to be there instead of here.'

'Yes, but there are compensations this end, as well you know,' said Jim. 'You have all the scientific help you need here. We're very primitive in comparison. This is the hub of all the police work and, being posted, you feel out of it. Methods change and more and more science is being introduced into detection. That's why I've got to come down here when I want help.'

'All right,' said Bill Austin, 'I'll think about it. This one is a bit thorny. What has happened to the shop? Closed I suppose.'

'Yes. I think the son intended to clear everything out but I asked him to leave things as they are just in case we want to go over things again. We'll keep a guard on the place. Mr Neilson accepted my request and was going to wait.'

'There is another shop?'

'Oh yes – Miss Thomas's. She sells everything at her price and I think that there was some bad feeling. Miss Thomas said that Annabel Neilson was undercutting her.'

'Was she?'

'No, I don't think so, but she was getting some of her trade, and I think that annoyed her.'

'I was just wondering. I had a thought. I'll be in touch,' said Bill Austin.

'Thanks,' said Jim and they shook hands. 'I've had some difficult cases but this one is most baffling.'

As Jim entered Paddington Station, a little bit out of breath because of his seventeen stone, he felt relieved that the Yard were prepared to give help when he asked for it. He did not like having murders or any unsolved crimes on his patch. He'd go to great lengths to clear them up, if it was possible.

Really, he was glad that he had left London. He preferred to live in the country and have dealings in a country town, rather than in a smoke-filled vast place like London. When he lived there he didn't notice it but now he was out of it he could not help but notice all the disadvantages: the noise, the fume-filled atmosphere, the speed, the fact that there was not a moment to live, all was rush.

Oh, yes, he was glad that he was going home to the slower life and being able to breathe God's fresh air. He preferred the smell of cow dung to diesel fumes. Yet he was glad that London was there, especially at a time like this when the burden of being the chief constable of a county weighed heavily on him when there was constant public concern about police performance. If a well-publicized murder was not solved, the newspapers would have a field day in speculation and criticism of the police. As the train rattled on through Reading, he dozed through the journey home.

It was music to his ears to hear the porter shout ''Ereford, all change 'ere for Abergavenny.'

He was home. It had been a long day, but it had been a profitable one and he felt relieved the Yard might find a way to solve the problem.

After three months back in the parish, Patrick felt that the place was settling down. The murder was becoming history.

154

Now was the time quietly to move to a happier atmosphere. The tension and suspicion still hung over Clehonger. The police in plain clothes kept a watchful eye and a listening ear like a barn owl silently waiting and watching for the slightest movement or sound of his prey.

Patrick changed his name to Watson by deed poll, his mother's family name, now he was starting a new life.

St Joseph's Roman Catholic grammar school wanted a chaplain who could also teach Latin and history. He applied for the post and was accepted. Father Patrick soon settled down quite happily in his new post and secretly he was beginning to form a liaison with a lady in her fifties but she looked younger. It was not long before they fell in love. It seemed so strange. Ruth Mottershed looked so much like his first love.

They had found a flat in the shadow of All Saints' church where their banns were read out and their marriage took place. Three days later there was quite an upset at school. Father O'Hara, their chaplain, was not there to start the school day with prayers. He'd vanished.

As they were trying to adjust themselves to the new situation, they discovered that Miss Ruth Mottershead the music and maths teacher was also absent and there was no one to play the two hymns for assembly.

How quickly it was news. The hacks were on the trail of a juicy tale of sex and intrigue. Days later the reporters ran them down to earth in a flat in Hereford, now married and seeking new work.

At last the battle with the church and with himself over celibacy was ended and the sexual relief and the joy of a loving companionship filled their lives with new meaning.

What a pity he had come to his senses so late in his life. He had been conned into believing that he was married to the Church. At last he realized that God had given him the equipment for a sexual relationship while the church in God's name told him that he was expected to deny himself his natural instinct which was God-given. It had been pressed upon him that he would be committing a grave sin by breaking his vow of chastity and would burn in Hell.

'What a bloody fool I've been,' he told himself. 'Now I am free to be normal.'

He had fallen in love with Ruth and this time he intended to enjoy God's gifts of sexual love and the joy of a loving companionship.

In his prayers he asked Annabel to forgive him. He blamed the Church for his twisted notions which brought about her death.

15

Never had there been such interest in what was going on in and around Gorsty Common. First there was the unsolved murder of Mrs Annabel Neilson.

Now their Roman Catholic parish priest becomes a school teacher and then he leaves the church altogether and gets married. It had happened before but it had never happened to the Catholics hereabouts: the shepherd leaving the flock to face the wolves in the guise of newspaper reporters.

The first reaction was shock and disbelief but soon it emerged that not all the congregation agreed that their priest had to be celibate. Mrs Williams, who went to him for his help and comfort when her mother was dying, saw no fault in him. Two reporters went to the wrong house if they were looking for spicy gossip.

'What do you think, Mrs Williams, about your parish priest going off and leaving the church and getting married?'

'I think he's a very charming man and I wish him all the best. The church has no right to stop him getting married. He's a man first, then a priest. If he feels that he wants to be married, I think he's right to get married. He's done a lot of good in this parish and most of us wish him well. Now you print that, it's the truth. We'd still like him to be our parish priest but in the married state.'

'Thank you, Mrs Williams,' they said. They had got very different answers from what they were expecting. The reporters found that there were strong feelings both ways but nearly all were sorry that he'd left them.

Patrick was enjoying a wonderful feeling of liberation. He might have been freed from prison. When he met Ruth the desire to be free to love and be loved was so strong that he knew that God did not order such a way of life for any man. Now he realized that he should have broken away years ago, instead of calling it a temptation to be resisted. He decided to act quickly this time and start a new life now and not leave it till later.

He realized why the church insisted on celibacy. If he were married, the wife would have some say where he was to be posted, which would rob the Holy Father of his authority over mind and body. It was a big con to control his priests. Now he had broken the wicked oath, he felt free from the fear of hellfire. He felt free of its power. As it rightly says in the Epistle to the Hebrews 2: Christ came that he 'might deliver all them who through fear of death were all their life-time subject to bondage'.

The power of love – yes human love, leads the way to a full-ness of life that he'd never had before.

They attended services at All Saints' church and soon they met the vicar, Father Charles, who welcomed them and suggested that he would like to introduce them to the Bishop. In a matter of weeks he was accepted into the Church of England and became a curate at All Saints' church.

While all these things were going on, Bill Austin of Scotland Yard had called together a large group of his men to discuss the Neilson murder problem. When he had explained the details to the Murder Squad, he wanted them to work out a scheme to break down the wall of silence.

Bill Austin wrote on the blackboard the important details about the murder:

The chalet was quite isolated.
It was very foggy on the night of the murder.
For several reasons it was very likely a man was the killer.

158

She was very attractive.

Could have been one of her admirers who was sexually turned on by her night attire.

He must have been well known to her. Powell was convinced he was local.

She made tea which they had in the kitchen.

Could have been attempted rape by the marks on her body and the terrible state of her clothes, which were torn to ribbons. There'd been a great struggle but she was not raped.

She was covered with bruises and several stab wounds.

Doctor said she bled to death.

Maybe she was killed to stop her reporting him.

She was killed between 11.00 p.m. and 3.00 a.m.

She was not expecting a visitor – she'd gone to bed.

Nothing seemed to be stolen.

'These are the basic facts,' he said when he had finished. 'The villagers are saying nothing. Powell thinks it's a local man. Powell also thinks that the local people believe it's one of them and they've closed ranks. No one is saying anything for their own protection.

'Go and have a coffee and see if you can come up with an idea to break their silence.'

They met again in the conference room after half an hour. Tim White was the first to speak.

'Say we have new evidence. We will have to fingerprint all those who have been interviewed to eliminate them from our enquires. That should worry them.'

Ron Perkins came up with another suggestion.

'Choose one of the most suspicious of the interviewed and make a big fuss about the use of a lie detector. They might want to alter their statement.'

Ben Grant's contribution was, 'Get the forensic boys to take blood samples to compare with the blood found in the house.'

Walter Bell asked, 'Why not interview some again and see if they contradict themselves.'

'Any more suggestions?' Bill Austin asked.

159

'Bill Adams, sir. Why not put one of the team in there to run the shop and be one of them. I think that they would like the shop opened again,' said the new member of the Murder Squad, anxious to make his mark.

Bill thanked them all for their ideas

'I have plenty to think about. I'll let you know my findings,' he told them.

The idea which seemed most suitable was to put in a member of the squad as the shopkeeper. He would live there and Bill Austin hoped he'd become 'one of them'.

Bert Longton was a Gloucestershire man and he seemed to be best suited for this particular post. He'd never lost his country accent which was very similar to those who lived there.

'You only have one year to do and I reckon it might take you that time to get the answer we seek.'

'Now there'll be four of you working on the murder case: George Lewis, Inspector Powel, Sergeant Smith and you, Bert, I'll make the fifth.'

George Lewis had already turned up some useful information about the missal which was pointing in a strange direction. This was still being followed up. But the local people were already losing interest in the murder. Other things like ploughing matches and point-to-point meetings and agricultural shows were much more in their line. Even the women were more interested in the gossip and when that dried up they reverted to their children.

Inspector Powell and Sergeant Smith were still openly working on the case. Now the policemen were liked as much as rats liked short-haired terriers so they drank in the Hereford pubs when they were off duty.

George had done a good job when he invited Father O'Hara to have a drink. When he handed the priest the small black book, George noticed the priest's jovial manner seemed to change as he looked at it and turned over the pages.

As Father O'Hara picked up his glass he had jogged his arm and spilt some of the whisky over the book. The priest had wiped the liquid off the missal with his handkerchief, before handing the book over.

As he did so he had said, 'I am sorry, I hope I've not damaged the missal.' George assured him that no damage had been done but he noticed that the priest had very carefully made sure that he'd wiped off all the fingerprints on the missal.

When the priest rode away down Birch Hill on his bicycle, George very carefully put the missal in a paper bag together with the priest's whisky glass and the ginger bottle and took them to Powell who sent them straight away to forensic to check the fingerprints. George at that time didn't know that Father O'Hara wouldn't be using a missal much longer.

Trevor Powell couldn't sit still while waiting for the results of the fingerprints. George's efforts had been wiped off the missal before his eyes but he had the priest's fingerprints on the whisky glass and the ginger bottle which Marjory took to the kitchen as George showed the priest out.

Bill Austin briefed Bert Longton about the situation in Clehonger and why he had been chosen.

'The shop where she was murdered is closed for the moment,' Big Bill Austin told Bert Longton, 'but it'll be an ideal place for you to live. You'll reopen the shop and continue to do the business as it was before the murder.'

'I'd be quite happy working in the shop,' Freda Longton told her husband. Changing from busy London to quiet Clehonger would take time to adjust. The shop would be a help for her, he thought.

'The local people will be pleased when the shop is opened again,' several people remarked. 'The competition has been very good for all concerned. The new shopkeepers will get a warm welcome.'

'You're used to this method of detection which has proved its worth over the years,' said Bill, his boss.

'It's as good as any, sir,' Bert agreed.

'I'd like you to look the place over and make your plans for moving in. I'll get in touch with the owner and we'll go into

161

business causing as little disturbance as possible.'

'In time you might find someone who will drop their guard and let slip the information we want. Call on Jim. He'd be happy to see you and he'll arrange to get together with George Lewis.'

'It'll be good to see Jim Matthews again,' said Bert.

'I'll write to him telling him you're coming. You can tell him that I'm getting in touch with Neilson, the son and owner, about the plan.'

'The son is willing to cooperate in any way he can,' said Bill.

'I'll go down tomorrow, sir,' said Bert.

Bill Austin's letter arrived on Jim's desk only just before Bert arrived. It gave Jim the answer he was waiting for. Bill wrote:

> I've had a talk with my colleagues and it has been decided to put one of our men in there to merge into the community, possibly to run the shop if he will. He's coming to have a look at the place, I'm sure he'll fit the job. He sounded quite happy about doing it. He can't decide until he's seen the place.
>
> Bert Longton remembers you and is looking forward to seeing you again. He'll dress country style so as not to raise any suspicions. When he has had a look round he will call on you and fill you in with his findings.
>
> Yours,
> Bill A.
>
> PS George Lewis can fill him in about the local people, and perhaps they might work together. Bert's a good man for the job.
>
> Bill

Jim Matthews remembered Bert Longton from years back. The Yard's idea might be the best way, he thought, provided that he'll be accepted as one of them, but tradition dies hard. The shop could help him there: a few sweets for the children;

162

not minding people calling after closing time; helping in the community. Little things like that could endear him to the villagers. If Bert Longton could work it like that he was sure that he'd get some secret information out of them. He put the letter in the top drawer of his desk. Jim hoped that he might take the job. It's a lot different from London. He might think he's being buried alive. I'll have to wait and see what happens.

Jim Matthews didn't know that Bert loved the country and would miss London like the toothache. The City air was bad and he hated city streets, the noise and the fumes, the hurrying people, all strangers to each other. The City offered an impersonal existence except for the few people you worked with but at the end of the day they all scatter to the four winds.

How different it was when he was a boy. He knew everyone in his village and everybody spoke to one another. This was an opportunity he had never thought he would be offered, and the best of it all was that he was offered a country job but was having a London salary. He would be working from the Yard, not from Hereford on a Hereford payslip. As he left his chief's office he felt over the moon. If it didn't fulfil his dreams, he only had one year to do before retirement. He could stick that, even if it was a bit of a bind. He said to himself 'Life is what you make it, and I'm going to make it good for me and the missus.'

Although Bert had lived in London for many years, he had not lost his love of the country. He was born and brought up in Bentham and his wife came from Ullenwood. The villages were only two miles apart if you took the path across the fields. It was there around Ullenwood that they did their courting. Freda Longton hated London but the job demanded that they lived there.

When Bert got off the train he looked almost out of place in his country clothes. It looked as if he had arrived on the wrong day. If he'd come on the Wednesday he would have hardly been noticed. He had been to Hereford once before.

Auntie Mary had been ill and his mother had been very worried about her. It wasn't really an outing for Bertie, she just couldn't leave him on his own. All he saw of Hereford was on the walk from the bus station to Bath Street and back again. It wasn't a very happy day for Bert, as he remembered it. Perhaps this time he'd wipe the old memory away.

Before leaving the station he asked the porter the way to the police station. The porter looked a bit puzzled at the request.

'The police station, sir?'

'I've got a friend working there,' Bert said and laughed.

'Oh, sorry, sir, it just seemed a bit odd going from the railway station to the police station when you've just got off the train. Well, sir,' he said, clearing his throat, 'you go out of the entrance here and turn left. There's nowhere right. Follow Commercial Road, passing the bus station. You'll come to a fork at the top of the street. Take the left fork up Union Street and Gaol Street is on the right.'

'Thank you for your help.'

'Glad to be of 'elp, sir. I 'opes you finds 'im all right.'

Bert made his way to the police station and was pleased to meet Jim Matthews again, now Hereford's chief constable.

Jim greeted him with, 'That's quick work. I only got the letter this morning telling me that you were coming. How are you? It's been a long time. You haven't changed apart from the bit extra in front.'

'Now, don't you start,' said Bert. 'Freda's always at me. How do you keep so young, Jim?'

'I watch my intake. I try not to sit at the desk too much and I chase the golf ball once a week.

'How long before you retire, Bert? It can't be all that long.'

'One year, which could be spent here. We'll see. Have you got an Ordnance Survey map of the area I can borrow?'

'Just a minute.' Jim went out of the office and returned saying, 'I have asked one of the staff to find one for you.'

'Thanks, that will help me do a recce.

'Can you recommend a hotel? Not too expensive and not too noisy.'

164

'It's no good me recommending The Mitre in Broad Street then,' said Jim Matthews with a laugh.

'B and B with evening meal will do me very nicely.'

'Well, there's plenty of those about, you should have no difficulty there.'

'How do you like being away from London, Jim?'

'I thought at first that I'd been thrown on the scrap heap but that feeling soon passed. You wouldn't believe it, but we are so busy here.'

'When I was at the Yard I thought police work only involved crime. Here it involves many things apart from crime, things like rights of way, market days and traffic control, pubs serving after hours. Wandering sheep and cattle, sheep worrying and stray dogs and, of course, poachers, and there are plenty of such people about. These are small insignificant things at the Yard but not here. They are part of country living. Mind you, I wouldn't go back to The Smoke for anything. Mildred disliked Hereford at first but she's changed her feelings. She wouldn't want to go back to London now.'

'I've been looking forward to retiring to the country, in fact we both have. Freda hates London,' Bert said.

'The Neilson case couldn't have come at a better time for me. My last year could well be spent in these parts. They thought that a man quietly settling down to live as a member of the community, as a humble shopkeeper, might produce the information we require to stitch up this murder case.'

'Well, it's worth a try. We've tried everything else,' said Jim.

A policewoman brought in a map and handed it to her chief.

'Thank you Doris.'

'Here you are, Bert. This should stop you getting lost.'

'Is there a bus service to Clehonger?'

'Yes, there is a bus every hour. I think it's on the hour.'

'It's funny,' said Jim, 'when you come to think of it. The bus station is where the old Hereford prison stood with cells, treadmill and gallows, where men spent years inside. Now it is the place where people can catch a bus to anywhere in the country. I'm getting whimsical, aren't I? Strange things do happen.'

They both agreed.

'I'll be off then,' said Bert. 'I'll see you later.'

'The best of luck,' said the chief.

Inspector Trevor Powell was still in charge of the case. As things were moving very slowly, he spent much time dealing with other matters. Sergeant Smith and George Lewis and now Bert made up the team to report back anything relating to the murder, however small and insignificant.

'I'll have to polish up my country accent so that I won't sound like an outsider.'

Jim laughed. He'd never heard anything so funny. All his men were trying to get away from the Hereford burr.

Bert introduced himself to Inspector Powell by saying, 'I've come to 'elp you, sir, in any way that I can with your case.'

'I want all the help I can get,' said Powell. 'I've had some difficult cases but never one like this one. I'm convinced that it is a local man and now there is a conspiracy of silence to protect someone.'

'They've sent me because my accent is like theirs so I might be considered to be one of them and they might talk.'

Bert left Inspector Powell saying, 'I shall need a lot of luck.'

'You can say that again, Bert.'

Bert caught the Madley bus and started his sightseeing from The Plough Inn bus stop. He walked round Gorsty Common making a few mental notes and saying good morning to passers-by. Country people speak as they pass one another even though they don't know each other. In the towns they only speak to people they know.

By midday he was starving so he returned to the pub from where he'd started his recce.

It's amazing how soon many local people knew that there was a strange man walking about the place. They couldn't make him out. His clothes and his accent were in keeping with a farmer but it somehow didn't ring true.

When he ordered some cider and bread and cheese, one man said to him, 'If you're not used to this strong cider, you'd better not drink much of it. It'll go straight to your head. You'll be all right if you eat all that bread and cheese.'

The others in the bar laughed when he saw how much bread and cheese he was supposed to eat. There was half a loaf of bread and nearly half a pound of cheese and a large number of spring onions.

Those who came into the pub all passed the time of day. One chap brought his drink over to Bert's table.

'Can I join yer?' he asked.

'Arrh, sit yer down.'

'My name is Len Waters,' and he held out his hand.

Bert shook hands and told him, 'I'm Bert Longton originally from Bentham in Gloucestershire but I'm not going back there. It's completely changed from when I knew it as a boy.'

'Everywhere's changing today, even 'ere. Some call it progress. I say it's a bloody shame.'

'I think you're right, Len. I'm just looking round hoping to find a place where I can settle in my old age. I like it round here and I like the people, what I've seen of them.'

'I'll have to go. Enjoy your stay, Bert. So long.'

Bert was surprised by how much bread and cheese he'd eaten. He liked the green cider. By the time he'd finished the food he wasn't hungry any more.

He went from The Plough Inn to find the shop in Hazel Lane. He noted that each house was out of sight from the others. The houses on Gorsty Common were scattered. They were built where there was water and the lanes wound their way from one house to the next. Since those days, the roads governed where the houses were built.

When he returned to Hereford he went back to police head-quarters and made an appointment to see the chief constable the following morning.

That afternoon he walked round the ancient city and

thought about the new job. He was sure that Freda would be very happy to be back in the country. As he strolled around he came to the Butter Market and a pork butcher's stall. He could not resist buying one of the pork pies.

'Yes, sir?' said the man behind the counter.

'One of your pork pies, please.'

'Which one? Six pence, one shilling or larger, sir?'

'The shilling one, please. I'll probably come back for another one tomorrow.'

'They're fresh every day. I'm sure you'll like 'um.'

'I'm sure I will.'

As he strolled along Broad Street he saw a sign saying, 'To Castle Green'. When he found it he sat where once stood an eleventh-century Castle, built to protect the city from the Welsh. He was glad that he'd bought a pork pie. He made up his mind that Freda must have one of these.

While he rested there on a bench in Castle Green, the whole picture of his future became clear and he realized that he was starting his retirement a year early and being paid for it.

He said to himself, 'I'll do my best to find that killer. I shall be more than happy for Powell and me if I pull it off. Powell's worked so hard without success.'

When he went back for his evening meal he told his land-lady, 'I've found a good pie maker.'

'Who?' she asked.

'Miles, the butcher in the Butter Market.'

'They are a very old and well-established butchers.'

'I bought one and ate it on a seat in Castle Green, and it was the best pie I've had for a very long time,' said Bert.

As he was eating his meal he asked her if there were any good films to see.

She looked at *The Hereford Times*.

'There's a western at The Palladium and *Ben Hur* at The Kemble.'

He enjoyed his meal. She knew how to cook, did Mrs Wilson, the landlady, and he was ready for anything including *Ben Hur* after such a fine meal.

16

'Good morning, sir.' Bert was right on time. He had always believed in being punctual.

'I hope you had an interesting time yesterday,' said Jim Matthews, opening the interview.

'Yes, sir,' said Bert. 'The houses are well-scattered in Clehonger. I thought that there might have been some sort of village, perhaps centred round the pub or the church. There are one or two rows of cottages but most of the houses are well apart and are hardly in view of one another. One of the attractions for me is its elevation, especially from Birch Hill.

'I had a word with an old chap up there. I remarked on the wonderful view he'd got. He told me, "I used to live in Birmingham." His accent told me where he came from. "When I saw the view, I decided to retire here. I bought the piece of land and had the bungalow built here. We've got a wonderful view and as the neighbours pointed out the wind as well. It doesn't 'alf blow at times. There's one good thing, it's healthy. The air's clean and there's no roar of the traffic. It's really a different world".'

'That chap you spoke to sounds like George Lewis,' said Jim, 'He's a big fellow, red-faced and his hair is turning white.'

'Yes, that's 'im. He was on the Birmingham city police as a detective sergeant for some years.'

'Anyway he's working for us now. He's trying all his crafty tricks to get information but he's had no luck up to now. I'll fix a get-together, Bert, and you can meet him officially. We'll go to his place and you can see the view from his sitting room. It's quite something.'

'It's so easy to rob or even murder someone without being seen. So many of the houses are isolated that anything could go on and no one else would know.'

'They don't see it like you. They're used to being on their own. That's why they're so good at doing their own repairs. They've learned to be independent and yet when there's trouble they band together. Like over this murder, they think that they're protecting each other. It makes the crime more difficult to solve. Although they live apart, they know a great deal about each other, not to mention many being related by marriage. That's what you're up against. Did you find the shop?'

'Oh, yes, thanks.'

'Everyone speaks, that's one good thing.'

'One old lady walking her dog didn't take long in getting round to the murder. She thought that it was a stranger. I pleaded ignorance, so she told me. Then I said, "Oh I remember she gave him a cup of tea". I put it to her that she would not have done that for a stranger. I didn't hear her reply. She shuffled off mumbling to herself.'

'I've given Bill Austin's suggestion a lot of thought and I've decided to take it on in the hope that something might help us in finding the killer.'

'I'm glad you'll do it. I believe, with Powell, that it's a local chap and the others are protecting him.'

'How do you think Freda will react?'

'I rang her last night and told her that I had decided to do it. She knew about the proposal and she sounded very pleased over the phone. Now I've got the feel of the place, I am pleased to say that the people are not hostile. They might tell us something useful.

'If Paul Neilson will cooperate, my Freda and I can look after the shop. We hope in this way to get ourselves accepted by the local people and maybe they'll open up with little bits of helpful information. The Yard will pay my salary,' Bert went on, 'and we'll do our best to make the shop pay.'

170

'There'll be no problem with Paul Neilson,' said Matthews.

'It would be better for you to explain rather than me, and the sooner the better. Then I can get started,' said Bert.

'I will see to it. He'd better come here and I'll explain the plan to him. One year will soon go,' Jim Matthews said. 'The customers will be pleased to come back. A shop is a good meeting place to pick up little bits of news.'

'I think that the information we might get in the shop will be from the ladies. The other good place I think is the pub. Between the shop and the pub we should get some leads,' said Bert.

'That's fine,' Jim said. 'I will ring you at the Yard when I have seen Paul Neilson. I'm sure that he will be quite happy about the plan.'

Bert caught the 2.30 p.m. train to Paddington. He was glad to get back to Freda. Whenever he had been away, the first thing on his return was to make love.

Freda was looking forward to his return dressed only in her floor-length dressing gown. Time seemed to drag as she waited for his familiar greeting, 'Hello, I'm back.'

First he took her by the hand up to the bedroom where she undressed him and after a shower they made love. It was always a wonderful experience. The magic and excitement never diminished. In fact, making love was much more exciting if he had been away for one or two nights. Whenever he was homeward bound after an out-of-town day or more, the train always seemed to have reasons to crawl instead of hurrying him home. But the reunion was always something special.

'I must go and tell the boss about the trip. When I've reported my findings he will tell me what happens next. I'll come straight home and we'll go out for a meal.'

'Oh, no we won't. I have something specially laid on for tonight and we will have it here.'

'We have already had something special.'

'Yes, dear, that can be repeated after we have had our meal.'

He took her in his arms and hugged her.

171

'I don't want to go to the office but I must. I'll tell you all about it when I get back. I'm not going anywhere else and so I shan't be long.'

He told his boss, 'I think I stand a chance, I know it's only a chance but I might find out something if it is a local person. It'll take time. We can take a leaf out of the Russian spies' book. The spy lives quietly and doesn't draw adverse attention to himself. He joins the local clubs and helps with the charities and becomes a trusted member of the community. The Russians have proved it to be a very successful way of getting information.'

Jim Matthews, the police chief, did not waste any time. He contacted Paul Neilson and explained the new plan.

'We'd like to rent the shop and put our man in as shop-keeper. Of course, Scotland Yard, as the tenants, will pay the rent.'

'It doesn't present any problem to me, Mr Matthews. In fact, it might be doing me a good turn if the business improves. The shop can be sold as a going concern.'

The local people had eased their troubled minds by convincing themselves that the murder had been committed by a stranger who wouldn't return, or as, the coroner had said, by a person or persons unknown.

Now the police were silent. It was their turn to be quiet and listen. That was the tactic that they were going to use.

The people who had been customers were highly delighted that their shop was to reopen and in a very short time everything settled down as before. Bert and Freda had found what they had been looking for.

In the course of conversation, it came up from time to time what Bert had done for a living before he retired. It was really only a casual interest in his past but it was important for his cover to manufacture some work he did before he retired.

Bert would reply, 'I am glad to get away from the noise and dust of the workshop. It was the bandsaws really which

172

created most of the dust and noise. I worked for a furniture manufacturer.'

Bert did a bit in the furniture line as a hobby and so it would not put him on a spot if he were asked if he could repair a chair, a table, a settle or stool. It's a bit tricky working under cover. One had to have an answer if asked, 'What did you do for a living?' A simple answer is quite enough as long as you can qualify it if put to the test. Soon he decided that he'd better have a workshop of some sort and so he bought a shed in which he could do the odd job. It was another point of contact.

He could always talk about woods, hard woods and soft woods: English oak and Japanese oak. He could talk about repairing things which had given him great pleasure in the past, especially when the grateful customer saw the repaired article and the wonder that came over their faces when they said, 'However did you do it? No one could tell it had been broken.' That to him meant more than the money he charged.

Inspector Powell had at last got the two lots of fingerprints: the ones that George had so cleverly collected and the ones on the missal which he'd asked for when he first found it.

When George offered O'Hara a whisky he told him to help himself to the ginger. This he did and gave a set of dabs. The other hand, holding the glass, gave another set of prints. The prints on the missal had been smudged, either by accident or on purpose, but the first set were very good. The ones on the glasses matched the first set on the missal. They were remarkably clear, considering where he found the black book. He now knew that the missal was somehow connected to the priest and there were no other fingerprints on it. George had said that it was a Priest's book. It was very mysterious, Powell thought.

After all this time, Powell was anxious to clear the matter up.

'The priest is in this somewhere,' he said to Smith. 'He's got a flat in Gwynne Street. Someone in the street will tell us where he lives. It will be the Reverend Watson now, won't it?'

'Yes, Sergeant. I expect they'll all know in the street. We'll get him to come down to the station. He might not want to talk in front of his wife.'

Mrs Watson answered the door to Sergeant Smith's knock. When Powell had introduced himself and the Sergeant, he asked if he could have a word with her husband.

'Yes, of course. Please come in. Patrick is upstairs in his study.' He heard the visitors so he came down to meet them.

'Good morning, Father. Is that right?'

'Yes, Inspector. I've changed churches but I'm still called Father.'

'I'm sorry to bother you but I wanted a word with you about the death of Mrs Neilson. It would be better for us if you would give us a statement at the station. We have all the equipment there for recording these matters and we can check it to see there are no mistakes.'

'Yes, Inspector, certainly I'll come. When would be the best time?'

'For us?' said Powell, with a brief laugh, 'Now, if you can spare the time.'

'I'll just get my coat. I won't be long, dear.'

'No we won't keep him,' the Sergeant said to Mrs Watson.

When they sat down in the interview room the Inspector said, 'I thought that you would be more comfortable here. I don't expect your wife knows anything about Mrs Neilson's murder.'

'No, Inspector, she does not, only little bits from the papers.'

'She did know that you were her parish priest.'

'Yes, of course, officer.'

'Did you tell her about Mrs Neilson's murder?'

'No, she knew about it from what she read in the papers. I knew Mrs Neilson. She was one of my parishioners but I was away from the abbey when it happened. My mother was ill and I was on my way to see her.'

'That would be the Saturday. The day before the night of

174

the murder. We came to see you in the abbey but you were away. The abbot confirmed your statement that you had left the abbey to go to see your sick mother.'

'Yes, that's right, Inspector.'

'Would you be able, Father, to clear up for me a little discrepancy?

'Before you left parish work you met up with Mr George Lewis. He lives on Birch Hill.'

'Yes, Inspector.'

'Do you remember him showing you a small black book and he wanted you to tell him what the book was.'

'Yes, yes,' he replied.

Father Watson was getting a little restless, not knowing where this questioning was leading.

'Did you recognize the black book when he handed it to you?'

'Yes, of course, I recognized it. It was a missal.'

'Did you recognize this particular missal.'

'No, I didn't, Inspector.'

'George, who is a trained detective, said he was sure that you recognized it.'

'That must be wishful thinking, Inspector.'

'Can you tell me, Father, if you didn't recognize it, how was it that your fingerprints were on it?'

There was silence for a few seconds which seemed like minutes.

'That must have been the missal I gave to Mrs Neilson before I went to Ireland. She probably took it with her to mass Sunday morning last.'

'Were you fond of Mrs Neilson, Father?'

'Yes, but no more than many of my parishioners.'

'That's very true by the number who attended her funeral.

'Thank you, Father. I hope that you'll be happy in your new church and new way of life.'

'That's very kind of you, inspector. I know now that I should have changed over a long time ago. I'm happy now.'

Bert Longton, now known as the furniture repairer whose

wife kept the shop, was sitting in The Plough Inn behind a pint of beer talking with Joe Morgan and Will Wright.

Will and Joe were well into their third pint and Bert thought that it would be safe to ask a tentative question, prefacing it with, 'I often wonder, when I'm alone minding the shop for Freda, who could have killed Annabel Neilson and why. What do you think?' He looked at Will and Joe as he said it.

'Difficult to say,' said Joe Morgan. 'She must have known people we didn't know, coming from away and all. Per'aps 'er husband wasn't dead, per'aps she had left him and he sought revenge.'

'This is something we'll never know,' said Bert.

'I 'ate to think the bugger's got away with it,' said Joe.

Joe was getting restless and was missing his poaching fun. He had been warned off poaching. The threat of gaol had kept him away from the poaching game for three long months. He couldn't go on resisting but he knew he daren't get caught again.

Nothing was said about the poaching for nearly three months. All was silent in the poaching world. Joe Morgan was telling George Lewis over a pint.

'Then we planned another raid which went badly wrong,' Joe said. 'We kept it to ourselves. We never found out how our plan was leaked.

'Me and the Turner brothers thought we'd have another go. We'd picked a field with so many rabbit 'oles it looked like a cullender which we decided to clear of rabbits for an ungrateful farmer. Someone must 'ave tipped off that bloody copper from Madley. It was as dark as a bag. Only the stars shone through the breaks in the clouds. Everything was as silent as the grave. The rabbits were feeding and with their good hearing they never 'eard a thing. When I got the sign I let the dogs go and damn me if lights did go up all round the field. I fell flat on the ground and rolled out of sight into a ditch. They caught the Turner brothers, but they couldn't find me. Not only had I rolled into a ditch but the ditch was

176

half full of water and I was soaked but it was bloody cold, I might tell you. I 'ad to stop there for a quarter of an 'our before I could move. A bad cold is better than a stretch in gaol. When I got 'ome I 'ad a stiff whisky and a real smart rub down in front of the fire and the wife was cussing me all the time she rubbed me with the hardest towel she could find, and it didn't 'alf 'urt.

'Anyway, I didn't get more than a bad cold and the Turner brothers were fined £100 each. They wouldn't speak to me for months. They laugh about it now. We're all good friends again.'

Slowly Gorsty Common was settling down to its normal uneventful existence. The Longtons were doing very well with Annabel's shop. The other shop had learnt to accommodate its competitor. What the customer couldn't get at one shop generally he could get at the other.

Bert had given up trying to get information. Nobody wanted to be reminded about the terrible event. Life must go on and it's as much as we can do to keep up with it. There was always the hope that there would be a breakthrough and the mystery would be solved. There had to be a reason unless the person was insane. If he or she had broken free from a mental home there would have been a massive search and everyone would have been on their guard. If only the police could find a motive. No one realized that better than Inspector Powell and Sergeant Smith and George up on Birch Hill.

They were all getting a detached view of the Neilson case.

17

'How's your leg, Bob?' Olive Taylor asked.

'Well, it could be worse, but not much.'

'You seemed to be having a bit of trouble getting up the steps.'

'It's improving, the doctor tells me. Sometimes I wonder but I keep hoping.'

'Anyone seen or heard anything about how Father Watson is getting on?' Bob asked.

'You knew that his wife had died?' asked Olive.

'Yes, I did 'ear. Very sad, him coming up to retirement too.'

'I heard that he's not moving away. There was talk that he might move but he's staying. He was so happy. He told people that he was much happier being married,' said Olive.

'I don't know how long she was ill but she died of cancer of the liver. She went as yellow as a guinea, poor thing. He was terribly upset. Elsie Sadler met him in Marks the other week. She was saying that he's gone quite old, she said.'

'It was a new lease of life for him, and 'er I suppose. She 'adn't been married before,' said Bob Evans.

'By all accounts he'd become a new man. Marriage was the best thing he ever done,' said Maggie Banks.

'I can't understand why the Church won't let 'um get married if they wantter.'

'It's not a question of religion, it's a question of order and discipline. The Pope wants them under his thumb not some woman's,' George said.

As George picked up his *Daily Mail* he said 'There's not much in it these days, leastways not much that interests me.'

178

George Lewis liked his morning paper and he reckoned the walk did him good.

'What's the doctor say about your leg, Bob?'

'He says that it'll take its time.'

Clehonger had gone back to sleep. Nothing very exciting had happened. Fred White had got himself married and he was now the proud father of two children, a boy and girl. He was doing very well at the garage. Now the place was all lit up with flashing neon lights in red and blue and green with a brightly lit up petrol sign for Shell.

He'd opened a snack bar which became the meeting place for the youth and they'd formed themselves into a club and Fred became the honorary founder member. His garage and showroom was becoming a Mecca for motorcycle enthusiasts. They liked walking round his display of gleaming machines with covetous eyes and the shining new chrome metal which enhanced their newness reflecting back the red, blue and green colours and the flashing Shell light.

There were Nortons, BSAs, AJSs, two flat twin Douglas's and a shining powerful Cotton. There was one Rudge Multi and one water-cooled Scott and one or two secondhand models in the background. The machine which took pride of place, however, was a brand new Morgan three-wheeler with a V JAP overhead valve air-cooled engine in the front and Fred was there to answer their questions. He was turning into a father figure.

Nearly six years had passed since the murder. Many still remembered Annabel Neilson and the brave opening of the new shop. Pat Watson, in his loneliness, also thought about Annabel. He still loved Annabel and really he loved Ruth because he could see Annabel every time he looked at her. He felt it was Annabel with a new name. He was so sorry for what he'd done. He didn't want to leave her, he loved her so much. When Ruth left him in death he knew what Annabel must have felt when he said he had to leave her. Now he knew that he'd done her a wrong and the sin of betrayal tormented

179

him and his guilt was getting heavier. He had been drugged by his religious teaching and only now had he come out of the stupor.

'Is he still in Gwynne Street?' Bessy Banks asked.

'Yes, he's still there,' said Olive.

'I'll drop him a line,' said Bessy, 'it might cheer him up a bit.'

'I'm glad we've bought that house darling,' Bert said to Freda. 'The prices of houses round here are going up all the time.'

They had had a bit of time individually to do some work on the house. One looked after the shop while the other went to do some work at Thruxton. Sometimes Vera would come in to the shop for an hour or two and they both could go and do some work together. Soon it would be ready for the great day when they could move in.

When Pickfords moved the furniture and all their belongings to their new home, Bert and Freda felt retirement had come at last. As Bert's working life drew to a close, everything seemed to be falling into place. Bill Austin was very satisfied with what they had done. Bert felt that he had wasted his time but he was reassured by his boss that he had done a good job.

Vera said that she would like to rent the shop and house if Paul Neilson would agree.

On reflection Paul thought that it would be worth more as a let than to sell. Will and Vera Maddocks met Paul Neilson at the shop and agreed the rent. At present, as Paul knew, the turnover was not very large, so they agreed to fix the rent for a five year period which was agreeable to both parties.

When Paul had left, Freda said to Vera, 'If you are stuck any time, I am quite willing to help you out.'

The day before the Longtons left, Vera and her husband did a stocktaking and they bought the lot and carried the business on as if no change of personnel had taken place.

Vera's little girl, Margaret, was into everything and Vera was not sure if watching her was making her old or keeping her young. The only time that she could relax was when her little girl was in bed and fast asleep.

'I shall be glad when she starts school in a year's time and for at least some of the day I'll be able to get on with things,' she said to herself.

The Scotland Yard Murder Squad worked closely with the local CID fellows in Hereford. Every so often a plain clothes officer would walk round the common at Clehonger and, once a year, specialists from the Yard would do the same. As the murder had not been solved, the books were kept open.

The Murder Squad kept a special file called 'The Unsolved Murder File'. Everything to do with each case had been collected, documented and all the reports put in chronological order. The Neilson Murder was no exception.

The first document was the long statement by Eric Willis, the local policeman, which included the statement of Ted Banks, the postman. Next came Inspector Powell's report, then the coroner's remarks and the doctor's how and when she died. Bert Longton's findings were also there, all neatly bound together and placed in a folder with a list of the contents written on the outside and titled: The Neilson Murder, Clehonger, 1952.

The file was put in the special drawer in the filing cabinet.

Where the murder took place was visited by a member of the squad every year as long as it was deemed necessary. Once a year an officer was detailed to visit Clehonger in the hope that someone would come forward with information.

'Sarge', can I have a look at the Neilson murder file? I've got to go and have a look round,' said Harry Paxton, a junior member of the Murder Squad.

'You don't think they are going to tell you anything, do you?'

'You never know!'

'You must be joking,' the sergeant said as he went for the file.

He returned with it in his hand. Before he handed it over he blew the dust off it.

'Where did all that come from?' Smith asked.

'I nearly had an 'art attack in there.'

'Why, what 'appened, sarge.'

'I couldn't find the damn file. I haven't been in there for months. The last time I must have been called away or something and I put it down on the shelf and intended to put it in the drawer when I came back and forgot about it. I nearly frightened myself to death. When you've finished with it give it back to me personally and I'll put it back in the drawer this time.'

'Anyway I'm glad it's not lost. I don't know a damn thing about this murder. This will fill me in.'

Harry Paxton took it to the restroom where he could read it through. He found it interesting. He had not known about it before he read it but he could not capture all the drama hidden between the pages of neat typing.

Clehonger was changing all the time. More and more strangers were building their houses and settling down and enjoying the tranquillity of the country life. The detective walked round, a stranger among strangers.

There was a time when everyone knew if there was a stranger in their midst, now it was a joy for one local person to meet another native.

Silence had been the predominant feature of the murder. Maybe they didn't know. Generally something would leak out in the course of time and so it gradually began to be accepted that they didn't know anything. Perhaps they were wiser than they were given credit for. They certainly never mentioned a single name because it was too dangerous, in fact it would have been wicked to have named someone by pure guesswork. The police would have hooked on to him and that person would have had no peace for many years. Now it was ignorance, for the most part, about the murder. Every time an old inhabitant died it was another potential informer who was silenced for ever. If the murder was mentioned, the reply was, 'It had happened so long ago before I came here. I remembered my dad saying something about it but I can't remember much. I didn't pay much attention. It must be nearly eight years ago.'

182

Old Roger Tomkins had just come out of the post office when he was greeted by Sid Bennett who lived next door to Roger in Gosmoor Lane. Sid had moved from Solihull and was very happy to be in the clean air of Clehonger.

'How are you, Roger?' Sid asked.

'Oh, I've been better many a time,' he said with a laugh 'I've worked on Morris's farm for years in all weathers and now rheumatism has caught up with me.'

'Oh, I'm not so bad when the sun is shining like today. I like to get out when I can. I've just come to post a card to my grandson, he's twenty-six tomorrow. I was just thinking as I came along how many great changes have taken place over the years. We used to make daisychains and pick cowslips in that field,' he pointed to some houses. 'Look at it now. It's a housing estate. The lanes on the common are lined with houses and bungalows fit for a city. The very atmosphere people came here to enjoy has vanished.'

'Of course, I don't see it like you, Roger. I've only been here nine years but there have been a few changes here in that time.'

'Hereford has become so near Clehonger today because of the improved main road and the motorcars and buses. The parish is almost a dormitory for the city.'

'You're right,' said Sid, 'and even the city is going to be changed.'

'What they going to do, Sid?'

'I've heard talk about building a new bridge next to the old'un. The traffic is getting too much for the old bridge so they reckon that if they take half the traffic off the old bridge it'll last a lot longer. The streets are getting clogged up with cars and the smell of the exhausts is no good for our health.'

'I haven't been there for some time now. My legs won't let me.'

'Never mind, Roger, you're still here. Some one told me the other day that you were an expert at laying hedges. There's very few like you about today.'

'We took a pride in our work in those days. Laying a hedge

was a work of art. They do it with a contraption on a tractor today.'

'I'll have to go. Now take care how you go, Roger.'

'I'm going back to listen to the news on the wireless.'

The young policeman who went to look round Clehonger knew nothing of the many changes which had taken place since the murder. The people did not know each other and some did not stay very long. If the staff wanted promotion they had to be prepared to be moved to other branches of their firm and sometimes their stay would only last a few months.

The visiting policeman could see the development because the old cottages stood out in strong contrast to the new and attractive new houses. These helped to turn the place from a country parish into an annexe for the city of Hereford. The very thing the newcomers were trying to get away from. No wonder the officer thought his chances of learning anything about the murder were slight, when more than half the people were new to the district.

When he got back to Gaol Street he said to the Sergeant, 'The best thing about it was the trip and the pint of beer ... with my lunch,' he added quickly.

'The old ones are getting less and less. Soon we shan't have to review this file any more.'

The young constable at the desk in Hereford police station got up and came to the counter and asked, with a smile, 'Can I help you, sir?' The visitor was an elderly man with white hair. The policeman thought that he stood about five foot eight inches tall with a slight stoop, in perhaps his late sixties.

'Could I see an inspector, please?'

The young policeman could not tell where he came from. He had a strange diction, perhaps from Newcastle-on-Tyne. Then he'd catch a word, as they'd say in the Midlands.

'What is it about, sir?' he asked.

The elderly gentleman said, 'It's about a murder.'

The heartbeat of the young policeman went a little faster.

This was something new for him. Was he looking a murderer in the eye? What could a mild old gentleman like him know about murder?

'Murder,' said the young policeman. 'Whose murder?'

'Do you think I could speak with an inspector?' he asked again.

'Yes, certainly. Please wait. I'll be back in minute.'

He vanished and came back with another officer, an older man.

'Will you come through, sir,' he asked the gentleman, holding open the door at the side of the desk.

The officer led the way to a room with the name on the door: Interview Room. It was quite bare and clinical: one table and two chairs. The officer went to the table and sat down and invited his guest to do the same.

'Please have a seat.'

The policeman was a friendly type who put those he had to interview at ease by his friendly manner. He looked in his fifties. His dark hair was receding but with an effort with a comb he was training his hair to cover up the balding process.

When he had sat down, the policeman gave the elderly man a warm smile and said, 'I am Sergeant Lindley, Can I help you?'

'I want to give myself up. I committed a murder nearly twenty years ago and the thought of it never leaves me. I have lived with the guilt too long. That is why I am here.'

Lindley had had some queer things happen to him during his twenty-seven years on the force but never one like this before. The policeman looked quite bland, although metaphorically speaking he had taken a right hook to the jaw.

'I'm sorry, I shall have to get another officer to deal with this sir, from the CID who deal in such matters.' He went out and knocked on the chief superintendent's door.

'Come in,' a voice said.

'I have here in the interview room a man who says that he wants to report a murder he committed twenty years ago. He seems a most unlikely person to commit murder to me. I don't think he's off his rocker.'

'What murder?' the chief superintendent asked.

'I don't know. He didn't say.'

'Well, you'd better go and ask him.'

'Yes, sir.'

The sergeant went to the interview room and said, 'By the way, sir, which murder are you referring to?'

'Oh, didn't I say? Mrs Neilson's murder.'

'Thank you, sir.

He returned to his 'Super'.

'He's talking about the Neilson Murder in Clehonger in 1952.'

'Now we know what he's talking about. This is a job for Powell. It's his case. Trevor Powell is in Tupsley. I'll get the desk to call him in.'

Inspector Powell answered his personal short wave telephone.

'Yes, Lily?'

'The chief wants you, back, sir, it's urgent.'

'I'll be there in fifteen minutes.'

'OK, I'll tell him.'

The officer Lindley went back to the interview room and asked, 'Would you like a cup of tea while you're waiting, sir?'

'I'd like that I think.'

Perhaps he's Irish, the policeman thought.

Inspector Powell and his sergeant were making enquires about a series of robberies which had taken place on the outskirts of the city. One elderly man was on the critical list as the result of the thieves' brutal attack.

It was a boring job and he was quite relieved to be called in over his personal radio. He thought that something had come up. Anything would be more interesting than this, so he was glad to get back to Gaol Street. The chief left a message at the desk to see them when they arrived.

'You sent for us, sir?'

'Yes, Trevor. I've got a man here in the interview room who

says he committed a murder, Mrs Neilson's murder in 1952.'

Powell's eyes lit up. He was holding back terrific excitement – after all this time, with a long line of cul-de-sacs.

Calmly, he remarked just loud enough to be heard, 'I've been on this case every since it happened and I had given up hope of ever finding out who did it and what really happened. I find it very hard to believe my ears. We'll look into it straight away, sir.'

As he entered the interview room he saw an old and rather thin man with thick white hair. They recognised him as the Roman Catholic priest. He was older and his hair had turned white, but it was still bushy and his bright blue eyes remained the same. He now looked rather pathetic. The inspector greeted the old man sitting at the table.

'We are sorry to keep you waiting, sir. We are kept very busy. I'm Trevor Powell and this is Sergeant Leslie Smith.'

'I never thought,' said the old man, 'that it would cause so much trouble before you could put someone in goal.'

'Well, sir, if we put an innocent man behind bars we'd really be in trouble with the public.'

'Who are we speaking to?'

'Timothy Watson, is my name.'

'And where are you from sir?'

'Originally I'm from Ireland, County Clare.'

'What do you do for a living?'

'I retired some eight months ago. I was a school teacher.'

'The superintendent tells me that you have something to tell us about the murder of Mrs Neilson in 1952.'

The sergeant got up and went out saying, 'I'll just get some paper and a pencil.'

The inspector said, 'You don't mind if I put a tape recorder on do you? It helps us not to make mistakes.'

'That's perfectly all right, Inspector.'

When the sergeant was leaving the room to get the paper and pencil, Powell told Smith to get the file on the murder.

'I was just going to get it, sir. I knew that you would want it.'

'Now,' said the inspector as he sat down, 'Please tell me all about it.'

'Well, I find it painful even after all these years but I do remember it all too well. You see, I fell in love with Annabel Neilson. She had lost her husband and had moved to Clehonger to start a new life. Our faith brought us together. We were both Roman Catholics.

'First of all I became a close friend and this went on for a long time and I believe that she fell in love with me and that she wanted me to marry her. This I could not do. I was already committed. I was quite content to carry on as we were. We were having all that marriage offered except the bit of paper. On the surface the relationship seemed to satisfy her but there were times when she wanted love and I was not there to supply her needs and so the question of marriage kept coming up and it caused disagreements between us. I'm afraid that we had some terrible rows and she threatened to expose me. I had to stop her, there was too much at stake.'

'Forgive me, but what do you mean?'

'My livelihood demanded no scandal. I held a sensitive post. It was late in November when I made up my mind to rid myself of this threat hanging over me. I told my boss that my mother was ill and I wanted to see her. I left on the Saturday morning saying that I was going to catch the afternoon ferry for Ireland. I changed my clothes and found a bed and breakfast place for the night. I said that I'd be late coming in so she gave me a key. I timed myself going from Hereford bridge to Gosmore Lane by the pathway and I returned by the road. Going by the path took an hour and fifteen minutes, because I had to walk most of the way. Returning to Hereford by road took twenty minutes. As the nights were foggy I added on an extra half hour.

'The fog slowed me up, but it hid my movements. I went back that night. She was in bed when I called. She let me in and we had a cup of tea. I told her that I had to see her before I left. She begged me to marry her.

'I did try to explain to her why I couldn't marry her and she became hysterical with grief and anger. I found that I couldn't do it.'

'I am sorry to stop you but you could not do *what?*'

188

'I felt that I could not kill her to stop her exposing me. I got up to go. When I got to the counter in the shop she came at me like a wild cat with the ice axe. I had to fight her to get the axe from her and my sympathy turned to anger. In the struggle I must have hit her on the head with the axe and with the spike on the other end I must have stabbed her several times. Then I realized that she was dying and I could do nothing to undo it. It all happened so quickly. I had done what I came to do but in those black moments I was both sorry for what I had done and glad that it was all over. Even though I had decided to leave the area, her knowledge could still catch up with me. It was then, as she lay there, that I realized I had to leave no trace and so I wiped everything I could think of which I had touched, including the cup and saucer. I knew that she had kept my letters. she told me that she kept them in the desk on the dresser. I got them and later burnt them. I took the ice axe with me. It was such a curious thing that I had asked her where she got it from and she told me she had bought it from a rummage sale and used it for splitting wood for lighting the fire. It was kept in the back kitchen. I've told you that, inspector, because you'd want to know about it.

'I left the door partly open as I left, to make sure not to disturb the door bell which would make a terrific noise in the silence. It was foggy which helped me get away. It was about two thirty in the morning and nobody was about. I went the back way past Clehonger pool, where I threw the ice axe as far towards the middle as I could. A moorhen gave a warning call. It seemed loud enough to awaken the dead in the churchyard. I hurried away, passing the village school, and took the Eaton Bishop back road to Hereford.

'I left my bicycle at the left luggage, having wiped it clean of fingerprints, and took my bag from the left luggage and caught the six thirty train to Crewe. There I bought a single ticket for Liverpool and boarded the afternoon ferry to Ireland. I went to stay with my sick mother for two months. She had had a very bad attack of flu but now she was strong enough for me to return to my English parish.'

189

'We will have to keep you here while we make further enquiries,' said Trevor Powell.

Another officer led him away to a police cell.

18

Sergeant Smith had found the file marked NEILSON MURDER, 1952 and the little things described by Timothy Watson tallied with the things in the file.

'I remember we had a cup of tea in the kitchen,' he said.

That accounts for the cups and saucers on the kitchen table. He gave an accurate description of where the body was found. He mentions the fact that the house door had been left open. No one but the murderer knew why the door was carefully left open.

'It looks as if we have our killer,' said Sergeant Smith to his boss.

'After all the trouble we've had I'm hesitant to say we have,' said Inspector Powell.

'A murder of passion, I said, as I recall, a long time ago, but how could we prove it?'

There were several new facts emerging and one very important item had to be verified and that was the whereabouts of the murder weapon. The following day police frogmen were called in to search Clehonger pool to see if they could recover the axe.

It was not very long before a crowd of people gathered round the water to watch the frogmen do a systematic search for the murder weapon. The frogmen had seen a copy of what it look like, so they knew what they were looking for. They moved in a line across the pool, leaving muddy water behind them and the people were able to watch their progress.

'Never before had anyone been to the bottom of the pond and no one knows how deep it is,' Joe Morgan said to Fred White, who had found time in his busy life to come and see the spectacle.

Under its placid surface all kinds of things were hidden from view: parts of old prams, cycle wheels, metal bed ends and bottles and among these once proudly owned possessions was the ice axe head which was easily recognized by the description the old man had given: 'An axe head one way and an ice pick the other way'. This was the thing that all the divers were looking for. The only time the people could have seen it was when one of the divers held it up for Inspector Powell to see. Within minutes Inspector Powell was holding the rust-covered object in his hand.

This was the very tool which was used to kill a beautiful woman so many years ago. In those fleeting moments, as he held it in his hand, the crime of passion flashed through his mind. Then the picture of a feeble old man who had used it on that cold foggy and fateful November night flashed into his memory. Looking at this saintly looking gentleman he found it hard to believe that he was a murderer.

The axe had been found. Soon the water was still again and the pool was left to hide all its other secrets. The police and the frogmen were first to leave and gradually the crowd also quietly melted away. No one was near enough to see the axe head. The police were treating it like lost treasure. The inspector carried it away with a look of satisfaction on his face. An important part of the murder had been cracked.

Trevor Powell, with the approval of his chief, telephoned Scotland Yard and reported what information he had. He was, however, able to tell the Murder Squad.

'We've found the murder weapon and it tallied with the description given by the old man in the interview, so now I am sure that we have the man who murdered Mrs Neilson in 1952.'

Chief Inspector Austin had been retired for some time and George Lewis and Bert Longton had enjoyed their retirement but they never knew who killed Annabel Neilson. The nagging thoughts about this murder which Powell had wrestled with for so many years were being unravelled like a skein of wool. Much to his mental relief, the matter would be cleared up only days away from his own farewell party.

'I am glad that I can close this enquiry. I couldn't have had a better parting gift,' he told those who had come to wish him a happy retirement.

'I had a very good team of helpers and I want to thank them all for their help. I must mention George Lewis. He was a CID detective in the Birmingham force. Circumstances made him leave his police work but he came back to it in helping us solve this murder. I'm sorry he's not alive to be with us this evening. Bert Longton is very sorry not to be with us. He did noble work, together with Freda, his wife, in becoming undercover shopkeepers. He's very pleased that we have a result for all our labours.'

Powell was nearly right about one thing. He was so sure that the murderer was a local person. In one sense he was right. The killer was well-known in the area but really Powell meant the killer was a native, born and bred in the place.

Powell was right with his other conclusion, namely that he was up against a person who was clever, calculating and cool under pressure.

Trevor Powell's message to the Murder Squad spoke of final victory. They could close the Neilson Murder file. The mystery had been unravelled. He thanked them for all their help in this most difficult case. It was now a 'solved murder'.

It was decided that Watson should be interviewed by two Murder Squad officers from the Yard. The old man seemed to be quite content to be in a police cell. It was noticeable how he looked forward to his meals. At least one person in the station didn't complain about his food.

The following day two officers arrived and sought to be enlightened on several matters. The inspectors from New Scotland Yard were very anxious to find out what really happened.

'Mr Watson, will you tell us exactly what really happened so that we can get the record clear?'

The old man was quite willing to go into his story in detail. He did say that it brought back memories he would like to forget.

'I had been having a relationship with Annabel Neilson. It developed into a passionate love affair. For a long time everything was fine until I realized that it could not go on and I had better move away, out of temptation's reach. The first time I dropped the hint that I would soon have to move she became very upset and cried in my arms. Because I didn't relent, her tears turned to tears of anger because I refused to marry her and she threatened me with exposure. The relationship was becoming very difficult. I loved her and I know she loved me but she was unable to understand my position. She thought I was putting her off because I didn't want to marry her.

'This last visit was my final attempt to change her mind. I had hoped that she would have accepted the situation without threatening me with exposure.

'She was in bed when I arrived but she was delighted to see me. She hugged me and kissed me and led me to her bedroom where she undressed me. I must admit that I was more than ready and willing to make love.

'I didn't realize at the time that she was trying to persuade me, as best she knew how, to leave the church and marry her. It was the most wonderful act of love I'd ever experienced with her. Then we'd held each other for a while and then made love again. Afterwards, Annabel made a cup of tea which we drank in the kitchen. She was still in her nightie but now she was wearing her dressing gown. Annabel turned the conversation back to marriage again. I refused and there followed another row and again she threatened to ruin me.

'I told her that I would be leaving the area. She didn't know it but this was her last chance to stay alive. She went into a terrible rage, shouting at me, telling me what she thought of me. She would tell the world about my wicked behaviour.

194

'I got up and I put my Pack-a-mack on ready to go and leave her. I found that I couldn't do what I intended to do so I was going to get out. As she came at me she was saying, "I've given you all a woman can give only to have it thrown back in my face. You have deceived me and used me for your own ends and satisfaction," and she came at me brandishing a climbing tool which she used to attack me and a fight ensued and I killed her. I intended to shut her up if she insisted on exposing me and she did say that she would ruin me. I had laid my plans carefully and was prepared to kill her if I had to. I had thought out every foreseeable problem.

'After the row, the silence of her death was almost overpowering. But it helped me to think clearly about what I had to do before leaving. I wiped all the things I could think of which I had touched, then I retrieved my letters from her desk so that I could destroy them, then I carefully pulled the front door to shut it but I couldn't without ringing the bell so I had to leave it open, but I made sure that there were no finger marks as I left.

'When I left the chalet the fog was thick, which for me was a mixed blessing. No one would see my departure as I vanished into the murk but it also made my progress slower than I'd would've liked. As I reached the end of Gosmore Lane at the bottom of the Bowling Green pitch the fog lifted a little so I was able to hurry my steps. It was too dangerous to ride. I left my bicycle in the left luggage to be collected if and when I returned.

'The whole question of my relationship with Annabel Neilson had been a great weight on my mind. Once the relationship had become physical the temptation became too great for me. It pulled me like a magnet pulls a pin. There was only one answer: to leave this place and start again somewhere else.

'I had been taught that if I let myself fall into an emotional trap, the only way out was to run from it.'

'You felt, that by moving you would break the pull of the attraction of Mrs Neilson?' one of the officers asked.

'Yes, the feelings would still be there but if I was so far away the relationship could not continue. There are some temptations in life, inspector, where the only way to break them is to run like hell. I told my superiors that I wanted to go and see my mother who was sick. Going to see her meant going to County Clare in Ireland. I was thinking of going to Africa if the worst came to the worst. But after that fatal night, while at my mother's I thought that it would look suspicious if I suddenly disappeared. I thought that it would be better for me to return to my parish work in Clehonger for some time, to lay any suspicions regarding myself.'

'Yes, I can see that. Continue.'

'On the Friday I announced that I would be leaving the following day, Saturday, and I would be going to see my mother and that when she was better I hoped to return.

'I left Saturday morning, taking my bicycle and suitcase with me. The week before I had been to Hereford and bought myself a sports jacket and a shirt and tie.'

'So you would agree with me if I said you had planned to kill her?'

'Yes, but only if she insisted on exposing me and ruining my life. When I arrived in Hereford I found a gents' lavatory and here I took off my working clothes and put on my new ones and waited a little while before coming out of the building a different person. Then I looked for a bed and breakfast under my new name Watson. That night I . . .'

'Are you telling us that your real name is not Timothy Watson?'

'Yes, I suppose I am, but we'll come to that later. That night I planned what I would do.

'On the morrow, Sunday, I'd explore the path by the river and see if I could use my bicycle on the short cut to Clehonger.

'There was a lot of fog about that November so it was essential that I did a recce in case the fog came down. It had been quite foggy in Hereford that Saturday night. I reasoned that not many people would be using the pathway in the fog. I did not see or hear a soul. When I reached the back road to Eaton Bishop I had no need to go the rest of the way that night. I would follow the road and turn down to Clehonger church and go along the path up the three fields to the Bowling Green Farm and pop down Gosmore Lane and I would be there.

'Sunday was a dull day and only a few people were about and I passed no one on the path between the Wye Bridge and Clehonger. I calculated that it would take me two hours to reach the top of Gosmore Lane, so add on another ten minutes to reach Hazel Lane in the dark and that would give me time and to spare.

'So I estimated that I could do it easily in two hours, even if it was foggy. In the early evening I took my bag and put it in the left luggage office, then I bought a ticket to Liverpool via Crewe and asked about the time of the trains and the frequency from Crewe to Liverpool. I made notes of the times.'

'Why didn't you book right through to Liverpool?'

'I thought that it would make it more difficult for someone to trace my steps. Now I had got it all worked out. If she was going to expose me, I would be well gone before her body would be discovered.'

'How did you intend to remove the blood on your clothes? There was bound to have been some.'

'That night I was wearing my Pac-a-mac to keep out the damp and the cold. I burned the mac under a hedge on my way back to Hereford. I told people that I was going to Ireland to see my sick mother. Naturally, they assumed that I would be going on the afternoon ferry to Dublin. Inspector Powell was told that I left on Saturday. I left the abbey on Saturday, that was true, but I didn't say I was catching the Irish ferry on Saturday.

'All these plans, which I had made for a quiet get-away from the place of the murder if I was threatened with exposure, came in very handy. It had been a successful operation.

'It may sound a bit strange to your ears. I believed that I was married to the church which was even more binding than being married to a woman. And to break that vow of chastity was the greatest sin a man could commit and his destination was hell.'

197

'But you broke the vow of chastity when you made love to Annabel Neilson.'

'I did not think so. I would only break the rule of chastity if I broke the marriage vow which I made to the church. If I married Annabel I would be breaking the vow to the church so that I could make a different vow.'

'It is a little too complicated for me,' one of the police officers said.

'I had to reason with myself that we have these sexual feelings because they are put there by God, so rightly I ended my celibate life. I realized that the church was wrong. God put these things in man and God cannot be wrong, therefore I should leave this priesthood and marry if I wished and God will not blame me. My war of pent-up emotion and desires are now over, but the sense of guilt will always remain.

'During my stay at my mother's I decided to cease to be a parish priest. When the parish of Clehonger was settled down again, I'll look for another post, I thought. I studied the work columns and eventually got a post at a Catholic school as a chaplain and teacher of Latin and history. While teaching there I met my future wife. We married and became members of the Anglican Church and I was accepted into their orders and my wife worked in a Church of England school and I became the assistant priest at All Saints' church in the city.

'I've never lost my deep feeling of guilt which gave me terrible feelings of remorse. I had reasoned it out that I had done wrong. I should have married Annabel but I believed that I would be wilfully committing a mortal sin and in so doing I would be cast into hellfire and my good work terminated. My spiritual row with the church exploded and I married believing that what I had been taught was untrue. I had broken out of the cage.

'There was a blank spot in my fight with Annabel Neilson. I still can't remember stabbing her, although I know I must have done. The remorse stays with me and my guilty conscience never leaves me.

'When my wife died, I decided to give myself up and confess to the murder.'

The two men from the Yard sat very still. One of them had taken notes and they also had it all on the recorder.

'Is there anything further, Mr Watson?'

'There is a little bit more.

'My real name is Patrick O'Hara and I was born and grew up in County Clare. When I left the Church of Rome I started a new life with a new name which also helped me hide from the law. I have always felt badly about the Church's rule about celibacy. I considered that it was unfair that the sexual part of a man should be denied me but I believed that marriage would be breaking the vow of chastity. I had been told in my training that I was married to the Church but I felt that I was a man first, before I was a priest. My vow and my collar did not save me from my physical urges. I did not consider that intercourse broke my vow, while marriage did. I would've liked to have left the church with its harsh rule but I had been taught and I believed that there was no salvation outside the Church I was in.

'I did not see the murder of Annabel Neilson in the same light as you, the police. I saw her not only as a threat to my ministry but I also believed that if I were put out of the church I firmly believed I would go to hell and at the same time bring my work for the church to a close. I considered that she was being saved from such a terrible sin by killing her. I believed that "the mouths of the wicked should be silenced".'

The men from the Yard were satisfied with the fuller statement. Many questions had been answered and many problems had melted away. He had bared his soul to the Scotland Yard police officers.

As he returned to his cell, the great banging of keys and slamming of steel doors impressed upon him that he was now behind bars.

The officers Sergeant Walker and Sergeant Mills were still puzzled.

One officer, Walker, asked Sergeant Mills, 'Was it really a guilty conscience which motivated his confession? He wasn't really cut out to be a priest. What does the church do with the naughty ones?'

'Puts them into a monastery on permanent penance and fasting, I expect,' said Mills.

'In that case, he's better off in prison. At least there'll be no fasting and no long stretches of silence.'

'He's no saint, this one, and no fool either,' said Walker.

When the old man was returned to his cell, the two men from the yard pondered over the confession. Was it really a guilty conscience that had made him confess? Or had Father Patrick O'Hara come to the conclusion that prison would be a happy place in which to end his days. After all, there he would be sure of three meals a day, a bed to lie on and free heat in the winter. He would have men to talk to. He might even be able to pray with the sick and help them with their religion. Perhaps he had felt that this would be better than living out the rest of his days in a silent and ice-cold monastery.